'*Fear* shifts our moral c
sympathetic to violent revenge, accessories
to murder. Do we want the victim to survive?
No, we don't. Long after I had put this book
down I still didn't. A great achievement.'
Herman Koch, bestselling author of *The Dinner*

'A smart, psychologically complex and morally acute
fable of modern German society decked out in the
garb of an intricate thriller.' *Sydney Morning Herald*

'An unnerving portrait of how close many
of us can come to committing unspeakable
acts of violence—often motivated by a fear
of violence itself.' *Lifted Brow*

'Dirk Kurbjuweit exposes the evil lurking just
below the surface of civilised life.' *Stern*

'Gripping, suspenseful and unbelievably dark…
As a thriller, *Fear* more than holds its own
against the competition.' *Die Welt*

'High-voltage and multi-layered.'
Frankfurter Neue Presse

'A subtle and engrossing psychological thriller that
gives an intelligent, carefully considered response
to the question of how much our liberal values are
worth when we feel our lives are threatened.' *Brigitte*

DIRK KURBJUWEIT is deputy editor-in-chief at *Der Spiegel* and divides his time between Berlin and Hamburg. He has received numerous awards for his writing, including the Egon Erwin Kisch Prize for journalism, and is the author of eight critically acclaimed novels, many of which have been adapted for film, television and radio in Germany. *Fear* and *Twins* are the first of his works to be translated into English.

IMOGEN TAYLOR is a literary translator based in Berlin. Her translations include *Fear*, also by Dirk Kurbjuweit, Sascha Arango's *The Truth and Other Lies* and Melanie Raabe's *The Trap* and *The Stranger*.

TWINS

DIRK KURBJUWEIT

Translated from the German by Imogen Taylor

TEXT PUBLISHING MELBOURNE AUSTRALIA

For Marja

textpublishing.com.au

The Text Publishing Company
Swann House
22 William Street
Melbourne Victoria 3000
Australia

Originally published in Germany under the title *Zweier ohne* by Nagel & Kimche im Carl Hanser Verlag, München, 2001
Published in Australia and New Zealand by The Text Publishing Company, 2017

Cover design by Design by Committee
Cover image by Cultura RM Exclusive/Atli Mar Hafsteinsson/Getty Images
Page design by Imogen Stubbs
Typeset by J&M Typesetting

Printed and bound in Australia by Griffin Press, an accredited ISO/NZS 1401:2004 Environmental Management System printer

National Library of Australia Cataloguing-in-Publication entry
Creator: Kurbjuweit, Dirk, 1962– author.
Title: Twins/by Dirk Kurbjuweit; translated from the German by Imogen Taylor.
ISBN: 9781925603033 (paperback)
ISBN: 9781925410709 (ebook)
Subjects: German fiction—Translations into English.
Other Creators/Contributors: Taylor, Imogen (Translator), translator.

This book is printed on paper certified against the Forest Stewardship Council® Standards. Griffin Press holds FSC chain-of-custody certification SGS-COC-005088. FSC promotes environmentally responsible, socially beneficial and economically viable management of the world's forests.

1

The night the girl fell from the sky, Ludwig became my friend. It was summer. The window was open and I lay awake listening. It was two in the morning. I saw that from the clock radio on the bedside table: illuminated yellow digits that clacked softly when they flipped over. Ludwig was asleep. When there were no cars driving over the bridge, I could hear him breathe. If a car came, I heard first a faint whistle, then a rushing sound, growing louder and ever louder, then softer and softer. Not many cars drove over the bridge at night. I strained my ears for the next whistle—I'd rather hear a car than Ludwig's breathing and the soft clacking in the silence. Maybe that's why I couldn't sleep—or maybe because I was wondering whether Ludwig might be my friend. A truck passed over the bridge: a dark whistle, a powerful rushing, the underlying drone of the engine—with trucks you always heard the engine, but only with trucks. I wasn't sure whether Ludwig was right for me. Then the girl fell from the sky.

◆

After school we'd gone to Ludwig's house. It was the first time he'd asked me back. We cycled to the weir, then got a riverboat. It was only a quarter of an hour's bike ride from our little town to Ludwig's parents' house, but he insisted on going down to the weir and taking one of the little boats that ran throughout the summer. We were the only passengers on the little white vessel as it glided, gently chugging, through the wide valley— green slopes to the right and left, fields and horse paddocks between them, and beneath us the river where we weren't allowed to swim. Straight ahead was the bridge.

To this day I don't know how many pillars that bridge has, though I often tried to count them. I'd start on the left, letting my eyes move from pillar to pillar, and would soon reach six or seven, but then I wasn't sure which one my eyes should fix on next, or which I had counted last. I'd start over again: six, seven, eight...Hang on, was it really eight—or still seven, or maybe even nine? It was enough to drive you mad. You had to stare so hard it made your head spin. I usually counted from the left, because counting from the right was even worse. All I can say is that there were fifteen, sixteen or seventeen pillars, pale concrete, sturdy but alarmingly narrow—too narrow for the wind, the big trucks, the four motorway lanes, resting on green steel.

I couldn't tell you how high the bridge was either, not exactly, though it was a question that preoccupied all of us boys a great deal. As high as the sky, we said when we were little, as high as Mount Everest, higher than a skyscraper. King Kong wouldn't need to duck, we said, if he was chasing us under the bridge. At first we used to say it was a thousand metres, but it shrank as time went by. Fifty or sixty metres was where we stopped, but I don't know if that's actually correct. It's hard to tell when you're looking up into the sky. It's high, the bridge, very high.

◆

I'd seen Ludwig for the first time two weeks before. In the middle of a German lesson, the door had suddenly opened and the headmaster came in, followed by a blond boy. The headmaster introduced him, saying that Ludwig had been sent by greater minds to help make something out of us. We grinned. We'd heard that line before. It was what the headmaster always said when a pupil from the school in the neighbouring town joined our class. The school had a reputation for being particularly demanding and the students who came to us had fallen short there. We never let them forget that they'd once given more cause for hope than we had.

The day the headmaster brought Ludwig into our classroom it was raining. We were reading Schiller's *Hostage*, but I wasn't concentrating. I was looking at the rain, the heaviest that summer, running down the windows in broad sheets. You didn't see drops, but curtains of water, and behind them a green shimmer—the chestnut trees in the yard. The windows were like lakes, I thought— vertical lakes, so clear that you could see the algae on the bottom, shimmering green. I was waiting for a fish. The doorhandle jerked, and we knew at once that the headmaster was coming, because he was the only one who gave the handle such a wrench that it jumped as if in alarm.

We were used to seeing our new classmates standing awkwardly next to the headmaster, their faces red, their eyes sometimes moist. The headmaster would rest a hand on the unfortunate newcomer's shoulder, and it always looked as if he was pressing them down to the floor. He was a heavy man.

Ludwig grinned, and I forgot about the rain. The headmaster gave us his spiel about greater minds and Ludwig kept right on grinning. 'Hello, little minds,' he said, and then he laughed. He laughed long and loud and bright. We didn't stir. We heard the rain and Ludwig's laugh. We were afraid, the way you are when someone else does something wrong but everyone is going to get punished.

Ludwig was about as tall as me, which meant medium-sized. He had a massive head, but you couldn't tell whether it really was big, or only seemed big because it was covered in such thick hair—hair so blond that it was almost white. A shade too white, I felt—almost as white as my cousin's rabbit. Ludwig's hair hung over his ears and was really very thick indeed, making him look as if he was wearing one of those Russian caps with the big flaps at the sides. But the Russians' caps are dark, and Ludwig's was white. He had a round face, rather a flat nose, thin lips and barely any eyebrows—or perhaps they were just too pale to show up against his pale skin.

He was still laughing. He stood slightly lop-sided, like everyone the headmaster brought in. That hand must have weighed pretty heavy on Ludwig's shoulder. It was only then that I saw he was dripping. He hadn't taken off his rain jacket—a thin jacket, the kind we all wore, with a hood. His was red. He was laughing so much that he was shaking, drops of water flying off his jacket in all directions. I saw one drop land on the headmaster's black shoe and felt even more afraid. Ludwig just stood there in a puddle of water. The headmaster looked at his shoe, and we all held our breath. Then he snatched his hand from Ludwig's shoulder, strode to the door, jerked down the handle and vanished. It was some time before we began to breathe again.

The teacher sent Ludwig to an empty desk in the second row, and we went back to reading *The Hostage*. It was quieter than before.

◆

Back then I was in desperate need of a friend. Having friends was all we cared about. Doing things with your parents had become embarrassing, and I didn't like being alone then the way I do today. If you couldn't tell somebody about something, it wasn't real. Friends were like mirrors, and we only existed as reflections. The longer your list of telephone numbers, the more important you felt. We asked everyone we met for their number and were eager to give ours. Then we waited for the phone to ring. It was better to be rung than to ring someone else. No one wanted to be the first to call, so we were all caught in the same trap. Despite all those numbers in our notebooks, our homes were very quiet. We waited. In the evenings, we counted how many calls we'd received. The more often you talked about your experiences, the more real they were. We wanted to multiply ourselves in order to be somebody.

Or maybe that's just how I felt. I don't know if the others felt the same. At the time I was convinced they did—to think anything else would have been unbearable. A friend was someone you could ring three times in a row, or even after every thought, every time you'd ridden your bike around the block. Only a friend could give you the uninterrupted feeling that you were there, that you mattered. And how wonderful it would be to be rung up three times in a row. I longed for it. I somehow hadn't managed to find a friend so far. I would circle the block several times and then ask my mother when I got back if anyone had rung. She would shake her head. I joined a rowing club—I liked the river. Swimming wasn't allowed.

◆

Whistling, rushing. People drove very fast at night. Ludwig had fallen asleep at half past eleven. Since then I'd been lying in silence on his blow-up mattress. I thought of all that had happened on my first day with him. His parents' house was directly beneath the bridge, or maybe not directly—maybe ten metres away. It stood by the last of the big pillars—after that came two shorter ones, because the slopes of the valley began to rise. It took us two minutes to reach the house from the pier. We'd leant our bikes against the fence and I stared up at the bridge. I'd often thrown my head back and stared up at the bridge like that before, but now I knew that there were people who lived right under such bridges, and one of them was standing next to me.

'A hundred metres, the highest bridge in the world,' said Ludwig, opening the garden gate. 'Did you know,' he said, 'that there's someone inside one of those pillars?' He pointed to the pillar closest to his parents' house. 'A builder fell in the concrete just as it was setting. They couldn't pull him out in time. Now he's stuck there forever.' He grinned.

I knew the story, but I'd thought the pillar with the builder in it was on the other side of the river. That's what I'd heard.

'Funny, isn't it?' Ludwig said. 'When you think there's someone stuck there, it's as if the pillar was alive somehow, because there's someone in there.'

'But he's dead,' I said quickly.

Ludwig shrugged.

♦

A living pillar, I thought, staring at the digits on the clock. It was good to have a bit of light. Sometimes the bridge looked as if it might move. It wasn't built straight but wound its way through the valley, a slight bend in the motorway. Something that's bent always looks as if it could be straightened out, or bent even further. If Ludwig had already been my friend, I'd have woken him now and made him reassure me that the bridge couldn't move. But he wasn't yet my friend, and I wasn't sure that he'd have given me that reassurance. After all, he was the one who'd said he sometimes thought the bridge was alive. The digits clacked. I wanted to go home. I wanted to get out of that room, onto my bike, away from the bridge, until I was home, in my own bedroom, next to my parents' room— leaving the door slightly ajar.

When there were no cars driving over the bridge, it was very quiet here, quieter than at home, where there was always a TV on or a door slamming in the neighbours' flats. A little before one o'clock I heard footsteps, creaking floorboards. Somebody was walking around the house. The footsteps stopped outside Ludwig's room, continued to the room next door, where his sister slept, stopped again, crossed the landing, went back downstairs.

I stared at the clock and tried not to breathe. It was twelve fifty-eight. I stared at the digits, waiting for them to click over to one. *At one it'll be over,* I thought—*it has to be.* My mother had told me that some American Indian tribes believe the dead return at night to retrace the paths they walked when they were alive—that was why you often heard the dead walking about in houses. *But never after one in the morning,* I prayed that night—not that my mother had said any such thing. It was an old house. *A lot of the people who've lived here are already dead,* I thought, trying not to breathe.

Soon after one, it really was over. Footsteps on the

stairs again, then silence. I heard a motorbike in the distance. Later I heard a toilet flush, a kettle boiling. I remembered that Ludwig's mother worked late shifts. She'd probably come home and listened at the doors to make sure her children were asleep.

Like everyone else, I'd been quick to get hold of Ludwig's phone number, so I could give him mine in return. We didn't remind him that he had once given more cause for hope than we had. We were overawed. No one had *ever* managed to make the headmaster leave the classroom in silence—and no one had come to us from the neighbouring town who hadn't spent the first two weeks skulking in the corridors, ashamed at having fallen short of greater minds. From the first day, Ludwig ran and shouted like the rest of us. Perhaps he even ran more wildly and shouted more loudly. His white head shone out wherever the biggest scrimmage or the worst fight was underway. But often, too, there was a great calm about him. I soon noticed that everyone went quiet when he spoke, which was unusual for us. I don't know what he said. I was keeping my distance, trying not to seem too keen. I wanted a friend, but one who came to me, not one I had to go to. I think that most of the time I looked slightly aggrieved.

I remember how hard I found it back then to accept that games had to come to an end. I didn't want to play football for an hour or two—I wanted to play forever. My enemies were the boys who soon ran out of steam or lost enthusiasm, but my greatest enemy was the dark. I even hated dusk, because it was then I had to start protesting, had to say that you could still see the ball perfectly well, that the way home was brightly lit, that our parents definitely wouldn't be cross—though mine were always cross when I got home after dark. I didn't want any old friend—I wanted one I could play with forever.

At home in the evenings, I didn't give my parents the chance to get to the telephone before me. I could jump up from my bed in an instant and take the two corners in the hall at a sprint. At the second ring I'd have the receiver in my hand.

◆

'It's Ludwig,' he said, the first time he rang. That was two weeks after he'd arrived in our classroom, dripping wet. 'Seven trucks in a row just drove over the bridge—that's a record,' he said, slightly breathless, as if he had run to the phone. I didn't know what to say. 'Hang on,' said Ludwig, 'I think there's another one. Listen.' I heard a rushing sound. 'Eight,' he said. 'Eight in a row—that's amazing.'

'Not bad,' I said.

'Oh, that last one was only a car,' he said. 'Oh well, eight's a new record.'

'Great,' I said.

'Okay,' he said, 'bye then,' and hung up. I went back to my room, lay down on my bed and picked up the computer game I'd been playing. Or perhaps I read—I can't remember. But I think I had trouble concentrating. Why had Ludwig rung me? Why was he so keen to tell me about the trucks? I hadn't thought much further about it before the phone rang again. I dashed out into the hall. 'It's me again, Ludwig,' he said. 'Four motorbikes. That's rare too. Funny day today.'

'Yeah, you're right,' I said.

'Kind of funny, anyway...' said Ludwig. Then we were silent. Silence on the telephone is strange. These days I can sit with someone in silence, but for a long time I found it impossible. I'd end up telling the stupidest or most intimate stories just to have something to say, and often made a fool of myself. I stopped as soon as I realised. Let others do the work—I no longer mind thinking my own thoughts when I'm in company. For years now, they've often been thoughts of Ludwig. But I've never been able to deal with silences on the phone, and that hasn't changed. I suppose it's to do with having a receiver in your hand. It's pointless holding it to your ear if you're not talking— ridiculous, even—and I always feel compelled to leap in with something immediately. But that day it was Ludwig who kept up the conversation. 'Do you think I'm an albino?' he asked.

I was quite taken aback, though I had, of course, wondered—I knew from my cousin that some rabbits are white with red eyes and you call them albinos. Before I could reply, Ludwig said he wasn't an albino, even if he looked a bit like one, because of his white hair and all. 'Definitely not,' I said. Then we both hung up and I went back to my bed and lay there, thinking even harder.

Half an hour later, the phone rang again. This time he didn't say his name, just asked straight off whether I wanted to go to his place after school the next day. I could stay the night as well, he said. It wasn't easy to convince my mother that there was nothing wrong with sleeping over at someone's house the first time you visit them, but I told her we'd become very good friends in a short space of time. 'Do you think he'd ring up three times in a row if we weren't?' I said. When she finally agreed, I was very excited. Overnight sounded almost like forever.

When we arrived, we went straight to the workshop. It was actually only a shed of wooden planks covered with a flat roof. The door was open and I could see a single-track hydraulic lift inside with a motorbike perched on top. A man was driving screws into the gearbox. Next to him, a girl sat on a stool, stroking a cat lying on her lap. I saw tools on the wall, a welding torch, a gas cylinder, a big barrel, a shelf full of cardboard boxes, a coal-burning stove. At the back were two more motorbikes, one of them without an engine, the other with a bent front fork.

When we entered the workshop, the man turned round and I saw straight away that it was Ludwig's father. His hair was grey, not blond, but it lay on his head just like a cap too. He had a thick, grey moustache with corners that curved down and framed his chin. He was holding a spanner in his right hand and gave an embarrassed smile. He said hello and then nothing else. I didn't understand—I was the one who was supposed to be uncomfortable, meeting a grown-up I didn't know.

'This is Johann,' said Ludwig. His father scrutinised the spanner. He was wearing torn overalls. I caught a glimpse of his underpants. He had a belly, but his legs were very thin. 'The cat's called Otto,' said Ludwig, and the girl introduced herself as Vera.

'I'll get back to work, then,' said Ludwig's father, turning to his motorbike.

I've forgotten my first impression of Ludwig's sister. I think I saw the cat rather than her. Vera was only a girl, a year younger than Ludwig and me. A cat, too, is only a cat for a boy of eleven, but I noticed this one, because it was filthier than any I'd ever seen before. Its fur was matted, and though it must once have been black and white, it was now black and grey. It had a greasy sheen—not at all like the shine cats have when they've just cleaned their fur. It lay on Vera's lap and purred, licking its paws while Vera stroked it.

◆

I thought of the cat as I lay in bed, still awake at twenty to two. They weren't good thoughts. Cats can seem sinister at night, and a cat slick with grease was so strange to me that I was convinced there was something peculiar about this house—about this family. *I should keep away from them*, I thought, and again considered creeping out to my bike. I was also slightly disappointed that Ludwig was asleep. All right, he'd held out until half past eleven—longer than anyone else ever had—but that wasn't the same as going on forever. Back then, I think, 'forever' meant until I fell asleep myself.

We'd played for a long time beneath the overhanging roof of the sheltered area next to the workshop. There were even more motorbikes there—half a dozen, all old and all from England: Norton, Triumph, AJS, BSA. They were in poor condition—rusty, gutted. We sat on them and played police motorbikes, racing motorbikes, military motorbikes, gangster motorbikes. We were so caught up in the game, I forgot about the bridge above us. But it was, I think, that summer that we had our first doubts about whether playing was the be-all and end-all of life. They were only fleeting—that flicker of hesitation you feel hanging halfway off a motorbike as you pretend to lean into a bend, going absolutely nowhere, a shrill screech—the noise of an imaginary engine—emanating from your throat. In the autumn following that summer, the autumn we both turned twelve, we abandoned that boisterous, unselfconscious play. That summer, we said goodbye to our childhood. Those goodbyes are the most momentous of our lives, and I'm very glad I got to know Ludwig in time to say them together with him.

◆

In the late afternoon, we climbed up the hill, heading for the bridge. The slope was overgrown with scrub and low trees. The last stretch was very steep. I slipped and fell, and Ludwig helped me up. It had been his idea to climb up there, not mine. We'd been sitting on the motorbikes and it had gone quiet between us. We were done with our game. 'Let's go up to the bridge,' Ludwig said.

At first I was pleased at this suggestion, which broke the silence, but then I felt uneasy. The bridge was so high, and the cars were whizzing past. I didn't say anything, of course—I just followed Ludwig, who set a brisk pace. It was a test and I knew it. I kept close behind him, trying to disguise my panting by breathing out every time a truck thundered past. Then we were at the top. We lay at the edge of the embankment and watched the cars. I was dazed and intoxicated at once. I'd never experienced speed at such close quarters: the noise, the force of the wind, the dizzy sensation when you tried to follow the fastest cars with your eyes and felt your gaze being almost swept away with them— the sense of danger. Deep down, I rejoiced. I was a trapper, watching a horde of Indians galloping by. I could have lain there forever.

'Let's go,' said Ludwig. He got up, slid down the embankment and jumped over the crash barrier. 'Come on,' he called when I didn't get up. I didn't want to—the ground was soft and warm. I couldn't. I wasn't allowed. A moment ago I'd been a trapper, but now I was my parents' child. Cars equal danger. A motorway is not a playground. A truck shot past. Ludwig spread his arms and was almost blown back against the crash barrier. He laughed. I got up and jumped over the barrier too. Then he began to run.

We ran along the hard shoulder towards the bridge. Somebody hooted. A hundred metres onto the bridge, Ludwig stopped, climbed onto the crash barrier and leant against the fine-mesh wire fence. I climbed up after him, not because I wanted to look down, but to stay very close to him. Even so much as a metre's distance would have made me feel alone. Alone on that enormous bridge.

Children have a clear sense of ugliness, but not of beauty. I don't think I was really aware at the time of the beauty of the valley I lived in. I looked down and saw the river and meadows and hills, our little town beyond them, and at its edge the dam and the small reservoir. I was trembling, scared of the drop and of the cars shooting past behind me. I was trapped between two of the greatest dangers of childhood—cars and falling— but I laughed and shrieked. I looked down on gliding birds. I saw myself high above the world with all its tribulations: my worried parents, school and homework, the anxious waiting for a friend. I felt bigger than usual, and older too. Being so high up made us grown-ups. Ludwig laughed and screamed as well, but when he said, 'Now the other side,' everything collapsed.

'We can't cross the road,' I said.

'Of course we can,' he said. 'It's fine. I've done it before.'

I was a child again, then—far younger than eleven. I saw myself running, saw the car hurtling towards me, the crash, saw myself spinning through the air, smacking down on the asphalt.

'It's too dangerous,' I said.

We sat on the crash barrier in silence. I knew how disappointed he was.

'I could have called anyone,' Ludwig said after a while. 'But I called you.'

◆

Ten to two. All I could see of Ludwig was the back of his head. I was sceptical. Was he really going to be my friend? I thought of his strangely white hair, his strangely white skin. It wasn't exactly a pleasure, having to look at that all the time. It hadn't been very nice of him to make me cross the motorway, either. That, at least, is what I thought at the time, because I didn't know Ludwig properly then. No car had come, we got safely across and safely back again. Even so, I was more frightened than I'd ever been in my life. But it felt great running down the hill with Ludwig afterwards. We made a list of everyone who wouldn't have passed the test, and in the end Ludwig and I were the only ones left.

I listened out, because I thought I heard footsteps again. But there was nothing. Everything in this house was different from what I was used to: old wooden floorboards that creaked at every step, as if there were somebody lying underneath, complaining at being disturbed; doors that only closed if you gave them a firm push or yanked them shut with a dull bang that made me jump;

shelves full of books with faded spines; small, wrinkled, dog-eared rugs. So much here was the product of chance: an air filter on a windowsill, a spent light bulb wedged between books, three coins on the arm of a sofa. Things absentmindedly put down seemed to stay where they were forever. In our house that kind of thing was unthinkable. My mother always tidied up, the doors closed quietly and the wall-to-wall carpet swallowed every sound. Our furniture was new, but in Ludwig's parents' house it was old, covered in thick coats of paint. You could see where it had dried in drips. The curtains had come adrift from their rails. It wasn't really dirty, but it was dusty, and it had a strange smell—the smell of all the years of living that had gone on between the walls.

Ludwig's sister slept in the next room. I don't think I heard her say a single word that day. At dinner she'd sat opposite me, next to Ludwig. Her father had the chair beside mine, but most of the time he stood at the stove, making pancakes. He ladled the batter out of a plastic bowl and poured it into the frying pan. Then he stood there—waited, flipped the pancake, waited again, lifted it out, put it on a plate and carried the plate to the table to slide the pancake onto the pile that was waiting there.

We ate in silence. At first Ludwig talked about what we'd done that day, but then he too fell quiet. We were fighting a battle. We were fighting the yellow-brown pile on the plate, a pile that went on growing and growing, though we ate and ate. We were fighting each other. We skewered ourselves pancakes with our forks, manoeuvred them onto our plates, smoothed them out, spread them with apple sauce and ate without a word. Pancake batter hissed and sizzled in the frying pan. Ludwig always helped himself before me, but I kept pace with him. His father brought another pancake. He was still wearing his overalls. I caught a glimpse of his underpants again. At some point I realised I wasn't fighting a duel, but a three-way battle. I'd been concentrating so hard on Ludwig that I hadn't noticed his sister angling herself a pancake from the plate in the middle soon after me—every time, without fail. I was confused and also a little annoyed. What did it have to do with her? How could a girl eat so much? I took another pancake.

I gave up when the cat jumped up on the table. Ludwig's sister shooed it off at once, but I'd already had an unpleasant whiff of engine grease and I couldn't fight on. Until then I'd been lost in a world of pancakes—the taste of pancakes, their smell, the sight of them piled up on the plate, the sound of the others eating them, of the batter sizzling in the pan. It had seemed quite natural to keep eating. But then I smelt the grease, and after that the smell of pancakes made me almost burst with disgust—a full, heavy feeling. Ludwig and his sister didn't stop.

She was tall and very thin, fair, but not as fair as Ludwig. If you looked very closely you could make out blond down on her face. It was a narrow face, her eyes round and grey. Her ears stood out a little—you noticed it because of her short hair—and when she turned to her father, maybe to see whether there were still pancakes to come, her nose jutted out sharply. She had a mole at the point where her right breast began to swell, but I have forgotten whether I saw it on that first day. She liked wearing floral dresses and left lots of buttons undone at the top, as if to show her cleavage, but she didn't have any cleavage at all then, and she didn't have much later either.

◆

When the clock next to Ludwig's bed flipped over to 2.02 with a clack, I heard a strange gust of air outside, followed immediately by a dull thud. Ludwig was awake at once. He leapt out of bed, far quicker than you'd have thought possible after the pancake battle he'd lost to his sister.

'Come on,' he whispered, 'but quiet.'

I felt slightly sick and too heavy to tiptoe, especially on those creaky boards—but we got out of the house unnoticed. It was still very warm. I didn't know what we were doing. I'd rather have stayed in bed, but I was glad Ludwig was awake.

He went on ahead of me down the garden, looking for something.

'There,' he said suddenly, and stopped.

On the grass lay a bundle. We took two steps towards it and I saw that it was a person, a long-haired person, a woman. My first thought was that she'd fallen from the sky. I could see that she'd come from a height. Somehow I had forgotten the bridge, though the pillar stood there beside us like a giant on night watch. I should have heard the cars too, but I heard nothing. I saw the woman and thought: *How could she possibly have fallen from the sky?* I looked up. The moon was a fat crescent. *From there?* I wondered. *How did she get up there?* I saw a rocket flying through space. I saw a woman wandering alone across the wastes of the moon. I saw her stumble and fall, fall, fall—a long, giddy flight.

'The second one this year,' said Ludwig, who was standing beside me. 'They love that bridge,' he said, and that's when I began to hear the cars again. Ludwig took two steps towards the woman.

'Stay here,' I said.

'Come on,' he said, taking another step so that he was right next to her.

'We have to tell your dad,' I said.

'In a minute,' he said. 'Come here.'

As I went and stood beside him, I suddenly thought of Kasper, at the kindergarten I used to go to. Kasper was a beautiful hand puppet with long, floppy arms and legs. If you put him down carelessly, as most of the children did, his arms and legs would fold at strange angles, and I always thought it looked as if something terrible had happened to him. I couldn't stand it—if I saw him lying like that, I'd pull his arms and legs straight. The woman looked like the carelessly dropped Kasper. I wanted someone to come along and pull her straight.

But it wasn't a woman—I could see that now. It was a young girl, sixteen or seventeen. She wasn't bleeding, which made it easier to look at her. Long, dark hair, jeans, a T-shirt. She had lost a shoe.

'Is she really dead?' I asked.

'They're always dead,' said Ludwig. 'No one falls a hundred metres and lives.'

I noticed how keyed up he was, but not in a nervous way like me—he was almost euphoric. He walked around the girl, bent down, brushed dirt off her cheek, and then, with one finger, he closed her eyelids.

◆

A lot more happened that night. The police came, a doctor, an ambulance. It was light outside before we went back to bed, but we didn't get to sleep for a long time. We talked about the girl, imagining what her life had been like, and why she hadn't been able to bear it. We suspected she'd had a broken heart, though we didn't yet know exactly what that meant. We argued a little about how long the fall from the bridge would take. Ludwig said ten seconds, which seemed far too short to me. He fell asleep after we'd agreed that the girl's name was Lisbeth. It was a name that suggested a life not worth living. Lisbeth sounded like sickness and death.

I lay awake a great deal longer—I'm not sure I ever got to sleep at all. I felt good. Ludwig was going to be my friend. He was eleven and knew all about dead people. Nothing had ever impressed me as much as the matter-of-fact gesture with which he'd closed the girl's eyelids. He must have done it before. I was at that age when you fear death more than anything, but not your own death—that seems impossible. We were all terrified our parents might die, because we were scared of orphanages— and scared of dead people, too. We saw them on TV, and at night they came into our dark rooms. Perhaps I realised that night that a friend is more than someone who'll ring you up—you need a friend to ward off fear. Ludwig could help me fight the worst fear of all.

2

Five years later, on a Saturday afternoon in April, I was sitting on a Norton under the roof next to the workshop. It was warm. I couldn't go in the house because no one was home. Ludwig had rung me two hours before to tell me I really had to come round. He hadn't said why. That often happened. I always did what he told me and it was always worth it. His parents had gone away for the weekend, and his sister was spending the night at a friend's. I'd been waiting half an hour. I no longer heard the noise from the bridge—I'd been at Ludwig's so often and stayed the night there so many times that I didn't notice it anymore.

When he did turn up, he wasn't alone. He had a girl with him, a girl I vaguely knew, called Josefine. They pushed their bikes in at the gate, let them fall on the grass and came over to where I was sitting under the roof. They seemed embarrassed.

I can't say much about Josefine. I think she was sixteen. At that point I'd never spoken to her, though I'd sometimes seen her on the street or at the open-air pool and knew she existed. Josefine stood out a little, because one of her teeth—her upper right incisor—was gold, and it glinted when she smiled. Perhaps it wasn't really gold—I don't know. Her family certainly didn't have much money. She was Russian, though our teachers didn't like to hear us say that and told us to say 'Russian Germans'. As far as we were concerned, they were Russian. They came to us from Russia, speaking either only Russian, or else a German that sounded as if it came from deep and distant forests. They lived on the housing estate where the English soldiers had once lived with their families, and we never went there.

Josefine had two brothers, who unnerved me because they had a reputation for wildness. I can't say for sure whether Josefine was pretty. Her face was round as the moon, and so was her bum. Her shoulders and arms made her look like a shot-putter, but she had long, dark hair, and nice slim calves and slender ankles, which I could see now as we stood under the workshop shelter below the bridge. She was wearing a frilly white blouse and a black pleated skirt that came down below the knee. They were the kind of clothes you'd wear to your confirmation—though not of course with gym shoes, which she wore without socks. She smiled and said hello.

Everyone said Josefine was simple. I was in no position to judge because, as I say, I hardly knew her. Another thing I'd heard about Josefine was that she was easy, but that shouldn't necessarily be taken too seriously. We were at an age when we had trouble distinguishing between desire and reality when it came to girls, and I wasn't the only one to have noticed Josefine's breasts at the swimming pool—or the only one to have fantasised about them.

◆

We were all waiting for something back then, and we knew exactly what it was. We had seen everything—we knew what a pussy looked like. There was a drive-in nearby and we'd often hang in the trees and watch the midnight films. The screen was four metres by eight, and they got up close with the camera. We'd talked it all over. Now it had to happen. We were seventeen, and reports were coming in every week about schoolmates who had done it—some of them younger than us. I'd sit in class looking at a girl and think: *Maybe she did it last night.* I'd try to work out whether there was anything special about the way she held herself, the look on her face, how she talked, or moved. But I was never sure. If I knew, I thought, it would make me a kind of accessory after the fact—only up to a point, but it would be better than nothing. If the girl I was watching happened to be sitting nearby, I'd sniff the air, trying to catch a whiff of her smell. Wasn't there a hint of something about Corinna? Didn't she smell different from yesterday and the day before? Somehow sweeter? It used to drive me crazy.

I wasn't bad-looking at the time. I wasn't particularly tall, but I was stronger than the others, more toned. I also had a reputation for being nice— friendly and fair-minded. It wouldn't have been too hard for me to find a girlfriend. The problem was the deal that Ludwig and I had made—not that it was a problem, not really. We'd made the right decision in agreeing to be like twins. Perhaps that isn't the right way of putting it, though. We didn't want to be *like* twins—we wanted to *be* twins. We wanted to be absolutely identical. But because we hadn't been born twins, we had to make ourselves the same—and part of that, of course, was going through all our most important experiences together.

◆

'Come along,' Ludwig said, and I followed him to the house, leaving Josefine looking up wonderingly at the bridge. He'd told her it was eighty metres high. No sooner were the two of us in the kitchen than he began to laugh and rub his hands together. I was soon grinning, infected by his glee, and it's even possible that I too rubbed my hands together. I'd sometimes catch myself doing it and be surprised, because it wasn't really a habit of mine.

Eventually he put a handful of condoms on the table. 'Are you ready?' he asked.

Of course I was ready—I was in a state of permanent readiness, though I'd imagined this would all happen differently. But Ludwig was right, of course—we both had to do it with the same girl, and as soon after one another as possible. We'd even thought about doing it with a girl together, but neither of us was comfortable with the idea. What I would really have liked was to have sex with a girl I was in love with and who was in love with me, but it was impossible to find one who'd fall in love with Ludwig and me at the same time. That was one reason we were so behind.

I looked out the window and saw Josefine sitting on a motorbike. I didn't know how Ludwig had managed to convince her—maybe she was somehow in love with us both. What did we know about Russians and their peculiarities? Perhaps we would both fall in love with Josefine that evening. Anything was possible—hadn't I found myself thinking of her bum some nights? I looked out again at her there on the motorbike, the oily tomcat crouched on the tank in front of her as she stroked him.

'I'm ready,' I said.

'I'll go and get her, then,' said Ludwig. He took one of the condoms and went out to her. I took the rest because I didn't want them lying on the table when Josefine walked through the room. Then she came into the house behind Ludwig, and I watched her climb the stairs. She turned briefly, and her gold tooth glinted.

It's hard to describe just how good it feels to know that right now, somewhere very close by, your best friend is doing something he's been wanting to do for years. I sat at the kitchen table thinking of Ludwig—not of what was going on in his room, but of the time when we first got to know each other—everything, that is, which I described earlier. I was glad to have such a good friend, and excited at the same time. I couldn't hear anything from Ludwig's room, but nor did I want to. I thought of Josefine at the open-air pool and of her amazing breasts.

I was startled when the front door suddenly opened and Ludwig's sister walked in. I jumped to my feet, though I had no reason to. She looked at me in surprise. She was wearing a floral dress again, and it's possible that this was the moment I first saw the mole above her right breast. She didn't seem to have changed much in the years since we'd met. A girl never changes, I'd say, as long as you look at her with the same eyes. Until then, I'd always thought of her as Ludwig's little sister. She didn't say much, and when she did, she usually sounded petulant. She still liked hanging around in the workshop

with her father, but she no longer sat on the stool—
she stood beside him, often with her feet in funny
positions. Either they made a big T on the ground,
or she'd be up on tiptoes. 'She's practising her ballet,'
Ludwig said when I asked him. I won't pretend he
didn't say it scornfully. I suppose that's how brothers
and sisters are at that age.

I don't think Vera and I had ever been alone
in a room together before. Luckily there was no
sound coming from Ludwig's room, but to make
quite sure that Vera didn't hear anything, I began
to talk in a loud voice. I said that Ludwig was up
in his room having a rest because we'd overdone it
at training, and it would be best if we didn't disturb
him. I was, I said, pretty tired myself—I'd been
about to make myself a cup of tea—and hadn't
been expecting to see her, as I'd heard she was
staying the night at a friend's.

'My friend's dad came home,' said Vera. 'He
left the family two and a half years ago, but now
he's back.' She shrugged. Her feet made a big T on
the floor.

'What, just like that?' I asked.

'The doorbell rang and there he was,' she said. 'With two suitcases.'

'What did your friend think? And her mother?' I asked.

'They were pleased.' She shrugged again. For a while, we swapped stories about parents separating, about divorce. We had quite a repertoire and often had conversations like these. My own parents had split up four years before.

It was a tricky situation. Ludwig, I knew, was upstairs with the Russian girl, and meanwhile here I was downstairs talking to his sister about parents splitting up. I'd been so close to getting what I'd wanted for so long, and now everything was up in the air again. Then I heard the bedroom door and Ludwig came down the stairs, looking strangely grave. He ignored us, walking silently through the kitchen and out the front door. I can't remember exactly how I got rid of his sister. I probably said that, seeing as Ludwig's bed was free now, I'd go and have a bit of a lie-down myself, or something like that.

Josefine was asleep—or at any rate, her eyes were closed and she started when I walked into Ludwig's room. I probably jolted her out of a dream. I think I was quite embarrassed. I stood in the middle of the room, two paces from the bed. She'd pulled the covers up to her chin and was staring at the wall opposite. It was some time before she looked at me, clearly wondering why nothing was happening.

'What's the matter?' she asked in her peculiar accent.

I couldn't speak.

'Are you scared?' she asked.

When I still said nothing, she smiled. 'You don't have to be scared. Come to me.'

I stayed where I was. Then she pulled the covers off and all at once she was naked before me and I saw something I hadn't been expecting. I'd thought we were well prepared. I knew what big breasts looked like when a woman was lying down—the way they spread softly across her chest. The dark nipples didn't shock me, and neither did the full hips, or the broad thighs, splayed on the bed. I'd seen all that before, at the drive-in. But dense black wool between a woman's legs—that was something I'd never seen. The women I'd seen either had a narrow strip of hair or none at all. Josefine had hair growing out of her groin almost to her bellybutton, and a little way down her thighs.

I was horrified and I was thrilled. Perhaps it made me think of something soft and moist and creeping, like moss. I'd always liked the feel of moss—I never saw it without wanting to lie down on it. I went over to Josefine, laid my head between her legs and kept it there, my eyes closed. Her pubic hair was soft and she smelt a little of rubber. Before long I felt Josefine's fingers on my head, combing my hair.

I lay there for what seemed like forever. Nothing happened for a long time—not much, anyway. When I finally lifted my head from between her legs, I didn't get far, because I immediately had to bury my head in her belly. I think 'bury' is a good word to describe what happened that afternoon. I buried my face between Josefine's legs, in her belly, between her breasts, under her arms, in the crook of her neck. I even pushed my face against the backs of her knees—but she was ticklish there and soon shooed me away. Most of the time I lay draped across her body, motionless, my lips or tongue sometimes playing a little with her skin, her hair, her nipples, her clitoris. And though it was actually only my face that was buried, I felt as if I were completely enveloped by Josefine. It was like lying in a soft, warm, damp cave, and I felt no fear.

We did it twice. Twice she called my name. Afterwards I lay beside her for a long time, my face in the crook of her neck. It was with a shock that I realised it was dark. I'd forgotten all about Ludwig and his sister and where I was. I quickly got dressed and went downstairs. The house was dark. I went outside and looked in the workshop. I couldn't find Ludwig. Long after Josefine had left, I sat at the kitchen table waiting. He didn't come back. It was well past midnight when I rode my bike home.

◆

I didn't see him again until training on Monday. We rowed a coxless pair. Perhaps I should explain: a coxless pair is a boat without a cox designed for two rowers, each with a single oar. Ordinarily, the cox steers the boat, but in a coxless pair you work together. There's a small steering system that the stroke—the rower closer to the stern—operates with his feet, but the more he steers, the harder it is to stay balanced. Because the rowers pull one on either side, they have to be well-matched to stop the boat from going round in circles. Ludwig rowed port and I rowed starboard. We were the ideal coxless pair: the same height, the same weight, equally strong, equally skilled technically, and we were friends, too, with the same way of thinking. In our first season, we'd won every race in the lightweight class.

In our second season we had new opponents, twin brothers from Potsdam. Twins, and especially identical twins, are particularly well-equipped to handle the coxless pair. We lost the first race and the second. The evening after the second race, we had dinner at Ludwig's, and when we'd eaten, he said, 'Come on, let's go up on the bridge.' We hadn't done that for ages—we'd given up play by then. I followed him up the embankment and we walked along the bridge until we were about halfway across. The valley was dark—we could see the lights of the farmsteads and the small town. There was very little traffic. Ludwig pulled himself up the fence until his hips were pressed against the rail at the top, and there he stayed. It looked as if he might flip right over in the blast of wind from the next truck.

'If I jumped now,' he said, 'would you jump too?'

'Come down,' I said. 'It's dangerous.'

I was just as despondent as he was—neither of us was used to losing—but it was no reason to kill yourself.

'Tell me,' he said. 'Would you jump too?'

He reached out, stretching his arms up as high as they'd go, until his thighs were pressed against the top of the fence. I heard a truck in the distance.

'Stop that!' I shouted.

He got down and grabbed me by the shoulders.

'You wouldn't have jumped,' he said. 'And it's true, losing a few races is no reason to kill yourself. But those stupid bastards are twins—get it? If we want to beat them, we have to be twins too. We can't crawl back into the womb together, but we can become more alike in our own way—more than we've ever been. We have to *do* the same things, *want* the same things, *think* the same things.' He was shouting. 'And if one of us wants to jump off this bridge, for whatever reason, that's reason enough for the other to jump too, right? Isn't that what you want?'

It was, and that evening I felt happy. We were friends, and soon we would be twins too.

◆

I want to make clear what Ludwig's words meant to me. We were sixteen at the time. We thought we were ugly, that we were repulsive, that no one wanted us around, but we desperately hoped that we were wrong, that there were others who might see us differently. At no other age do such great doubts and such high hopes follow in such quick succession—it's almost unbearable. And then someone comes along and says: *I want to be just like you*. What an incredible feeling that is! We were so unsure of ourselves that everyone else was a threat. Whenever you saw anyone in a new jacket, you wondered whether it meant a death sentence for all your jackets—whether you, too, didn't have to have that jacket immediately. We listened to every word the others said, how they said it, their exact intonation, trying to work out whether we'd found the new word, the cool word, the right way to say it. We had to be fast—we were always anxious, always vigilant. Having a twin—someone who never undermines you, because whatever he does or says or wears is always yours too—would free you from that constant anxiety. I think that's what Ludwig was getting at.

From then on I went home only to sleep, and sometimes not even that. We spent almost every waking moment together, watching TV, playing the same computer games, reading the same books, eating the same size servings of the same meals, and sharing all our thoughts. We lost another two races, but then we won all the rest that season. That was the year before we did it with Josefine.

◆

'I rang you a few times,' I said as we changed for training.

'I wasn't in,' he said.

The boathouse was small and cramped—there weren't even changing rooms. We changed in the workshop, which smelled of sweat and rowlock grease. Our weights room was there too, though we only had a beer-tent bench and a barbell with rusty weights—and, hanging from the ceiling, a wooden plank we were supposed to touch when we did straight jumps. There were a dozen boats in the boatshed, old clinker-built rowing boats for the most part, two or three plastic racing skiffs and our coxless pair—the only new boat. It had been bought especially for us, because we were the club's only true talent. There was also a small speedboat for the trainers, but we usually went out without a trainer and did our own thing.

We carried our boat to the river, lowered it into the water, laid the oars in the rowlocks, got in and pushed off from the jetty. Ludwig was the stroke and sat with his back to me. We planned to row a long way that day, ten kilometres, at a high stroke rate. We could row east or west. Rowing west took longer because the weir lay that way, and we had to go through the lock first. We usually went west anyway, because we both felt the pull of the bridge that was waiting for us in that direction. If we didn't meet the riverboat, we had the river to ourselves. The rowlocks creaked, the water lapped the oars. A grey river between green banks. As we passed under the bridge, we both glanced up.

◆

At milestone 43/7 I saw Josefine sitting on the bank. She was wearing her confirmation clothes again and she smiled at me, her gold tooth flashing in the sun. I was glad to see her. I had thought of her all day Sunday and was bursting to tell Ludwig what it had been like with her and to hear how it had gone for him.

'You're rocking the boat,' Ludwig hissed. 'Concentrate.'

I hadn't even turned my head—I'd only looked at Josefine out of the corner of my eye, though naturally she was occupying my thoughts. When I think about it, I suppose Ludwig's warning was a sign that we were growing closer, becoming more like twins. He sensed even the smallest changes, and that was as it should be. And he was right, of course. We were training—we didn't want any distraction.

When we were back at the weir, panting heavily, our breath perfectly in time, our oars lying on the water, Ludwig said, 'You'd better forget that Russian slut—she's not worth bothering with.' We'd just rowed ten kilometres flat out and were completely shattered, and perhaps Ludwig was still a bit annoyed with me for losing focus, even if it was only for a moment, so I don't think you can read too much into what he said that day.

◆

I tried to put Josefine from my mind. I saw her another couple of times on the riverbank, but after that I didn't see her again. Perhaps she was waiting for me to approach her—I've got no idea. It's true, we'd had a good time together, but what did that mean? I forgot about her in the end—I suppose we were really too different anyway. But something lingered, something you might describe as a general feeling of longing, the desire for a similar experience, though not with Josefine—no, there were so many other girls. But whenever I brought it up, Ludwig immediately changed the subject. Not that he'd been all that different in the past—he'd never shown much interest in such things. Perhaps it was because of me that he'd brought Josefine round that day. All the more reason to be grateful to him. I tried to suppress my longing, and for a time I was pretty successful.

3

When summer began, the weather suddenly turned cold and wet. Some days the temperature was just fifteen degrees. We were never dressed warmly enough and often soaked to the skin. 'What ever happened to global warming?' Ludwig asked, and we laughed. We laughed a lot in those days. We had it good—I think I can speak for Ludwig too there. I've never cared so little about bad weather.

I remember us taking refuge in a bus shelter one day when we were caught out by a sudden shower. Then, just as the rain really began to pelt down, Ludwig took three steps out into the open and stopped in the middle of the road.

'I protest,' he yelled at the sky. 'I won't budge until the rain stops!'

I went to join him. 'I protest too,' I yelled, and was soon dripping wet.

When the rain stopped ten minutes later, Ludwig yelled, 'Victory!' and I too yelled, 'Victory!' and we laughed and jumped in the puddles. I'll never forget Ludwig grabbing me by the shoulders, water streaming down his face, rivulets running from his hair into his eyes. When he yelled, 'We've made it, we've won,' the water even ran into his mouth. He looked happy—the way he looked when we'd won a victory over the real twins, only wetter. I yelled, 'We showed him—he won't try that again,' and Ludwig stuck his middle finger up at the sky. We didn't notice the bus coming towards us until the driver honked the horn, and then we jumped on our bikes and sped off, still laughing. In July the weather improved, and we told each other more than once that if you just put up a proper fight, everything would come right in the end.

We'd become twins—there was no question of that. We always met five minutes before school started—or rather, we always went to lessons five minutes late—because we'd agreed to tell each other our dreams every morning. Neither of us was a great dreamer, and I'm still not. We often had nothing to tell each other—occasionally, perhaps, something evil at our heels, or an embarrassing scene in front of the class, but that was rare. Every now and again, though, I'd dream of somebody swinging through a big top on a trapeze. When I climbed a rope ladder into the dome, I saw that it was Josefine, more or less naked, and we fell into the net together. Ludwig never had anything to say about that particular dream. Most of the time we didn't talk about dreams at all, because we hadn't dreamed anything. We just talked—about school or rowing or whatever.

◆

On one occasion we had a bit of trouble with Josefine's brothers. They wanted something from us—I can't remember what. The two of them were shouting and carrying on—they were crazy, like all Russians—and we ignored them for a while, until suddenly Ludwig hit the older one in the face. Without thinking about it, I immediately did the same to the younger one. He was so taken aback that I was able to get the better of him, and soon he was lying on the ground beneath me, motionless. I saw that Ludwig was also finished with his opponent—and I saw him get up and kick him in the side. Not hard—I don't want to give the wrong impression. It was a harmless kick—more of a prod with the tip of his shoe—so I don't mind admitting that my Russian also got a little kick in the side. They really were animals.

◆

We didn't mind going to school. We did well enough without having to try too hard, sometimes interested in what we were taught, more often bored by it, but never sullen. We did our best to put up with our teachers, who were touchingly serious about their task of preparing us for the adult world, though none of them could know what kind of a world it would be by the time we got there.

It was a time of uncertainty, of constant flux. The Wall had come down, the Cold War had ended, and now everything was shifting and changing. Our geography teacher was a monster, with a penchant for inflicting ridiculously time-consuming homework, but when we saw him standing helpless in front of the big roller maps at the front of the classroom, all their boundaries out of date again, we felt almost sorry for him. He would try to amend them, copying from maps in the newspaper with a thick black pen that he held in a trembling hand, but the result was invariably even further removed from the current state of affairs than the original map, because the pen always slipped—the maps were hanging, not lying flat. In his attempt to break up Yugoslavia in front of the class, he split the Greek mainland in two, and on another occasion he tried to dissolve the Soviet Union and ended up creating an independent republic in a corner of Iran. I never had an atlas in which all the borders were correct.

As for the computers we were given to work with, I don't even want to get started on them. In my final year I was still tapping away at the same machine as in the first year, but the time I had to wait after entering commands seemed far longer, because by then we were using much faster computers at home. Looking back, things at school moved at too leisurely a pace, compared with the speed of the age we were living in, to present any sort of challenge, and that's probably why Ludwig and I didn't mind it all that much.

During break we kept to ourselves. We had a corner of our own on the front steps where smoking was permitted. We didn't smoke, just sat and talked—to each other, of course. What would we have said to anyone else? The others got in our way. We had no need for them. There was, though, a brief phase when there were three of us. It began when Marco came to our school.

I knew Marco from Berlin, where we'd been to the same primary school. When I moved with my parents to the small town by the reservoir, Marco and I had written to each other a couple of times, but we'd soon lost contact. Then, during the first winter that Ludwig and I were twins, Marco suddenly appeared in the schoolyard one day. I recognised him at once and was pleased to see him. His parents had moved too—he was new and insecure, and I took him under my wing.

At break Marco sat on the steps with Ludwig and me, and I took him rowing and sometimes round to Ludwig's. He was cheerful and easygoing, and we had a lot of good memories in common, but after two or three weeks, Ludwig asked me if I didn't agree that Marco was too stupid to be friends with us. I had to admit that he was right. That was the brilliant thing about us—we always thought the same thing at the same time. It was usually Ludwig who was the first to put it into words, just because he talked more than I did. It must have been awful for Marco when we told him he had to find other friends, but I did it gently, trying not to hurt his feelings, and it wasn't long before we began to see him with fat Georg. The two of them later left school early and went off to join the police.

Vera was also at our school by then, but she never sat with us—brothers and sisters didn't hang out together. I have to admit, I really liked her. She wore her hair even shorter and her floral dresses hung nicely from her square shoulders. She no longer stood on tiptoes—at fifteen, that would have been silly—but she still stood with her feet in a T shape.

Once, in early summer, when it was still cold, I briefly got close to her. It was when a girl in first year was kidnapped. A lot of rich people lived in our town—because it's so beautiful, I suppose, with the river and all the greenery, but not too far from bigger towns and cities. A lot of the students at our school came from these wealthy families—their parents were executives and professionals, and they had pools in their backyards that they swam in every morning to improve their posture. We called them 'spoilt brats' and wouldn't have anything to do with them, but of course we felt sorry for the little girl when she was snatched on her way to school.

The kidnappers asked for three million. It was an uneasy time—police all over the school and on the streets. We all dreamed of finding the girl, of overpowering the kidnappers and receiving a generous reward. Ludwig and I spent a lot of time riding our bikes around the woods, hoping to uncover some clue, cooking up schemes to catch the gangsters. Secretly, too, in spite of our horror, I suppose we all sometimes wished we were in the girl's place—forlorn objects of pity. (And didn't the captive get first shot at taking out the gangsters and becoming a hero?) I have to admit, though, that I don't really know if this was something everyone dreamed of, because no one would have owned up to it, of course. I can only speak for Ludwig and me, because as twins we could tell each other even the most embarrassing things.

After three weeks, the ransom was paid and the girl released. We couldn't believe it when we heard where she'd been hidden. One of the shorter pillars hugging the slope on our side of the bridge was partly hollow. We knew that—there was a steel door, and behind it, we supposed, a storeroom where the workers who maintained the bridge kept their tools. We'd sometimes rattled at this door in the past, but it had always been locked, and eventually we'd forgotten all about it. It was in this storeroom that the girl had been kept for three weeks. We went to check it out as soon as we heard the news on the radio. Everything was cordoned off, and men were milling about, agitated. We sat up till late that night in Ludwig's room, trying to imagine what it must be like, living in a dark storeroom like that for three weeks, pondering possible means of rescue. It was frustrating to think that the answer had been so close at hand all along—the bridge was our territory, but for three whole weeks we hadn't had a clue what was going on there.

I didn't leave Ludwig's house until after midnight. As I made my way past his father's workshop, I saw that the light was on. The door was open a crack, and I heard something that sounded like whimpering or soft crying, so I stopped. Then I went to the door and peered through the crack. I saw Vera sitting on a stool beside the oil drum, her arms wrapped around her knees, her head resting on her arms. Her back was heaving. My first impulse was to slip away, because I didn't know how to deal with a crying girl, but in the end I went in. Vera heard me and looked up. You could see that she'd been crying for a while.

'She was in there on her own all that time,' she sobbed, 'not even a hundred metres from here, in the dark. She must have been so scared.'

Vera was a little ugly at that moment—big red eyes, hollow cheeks, her face streaked with tears. She looked like a baby owl that had been pushed out of the nest early. She started to cry again. I went over to her and put a hand on her hair. When she didn't stop crying, I moved a little closer and pressed her head gently against my belly. It was funny, standing there like that and feeling a girl's head on my belly.

'She must have been starving,' Vera sobbed, and I noticed that my shirt was getting wet. She stood up, wrapped her arms around my neck and laid her head on my chest. I don't know exactly where I had my hands. I seem to remember touching her shoulders, her head and her neck, and putting my hands on her hips, too. It was so strange—if I'm not mistaken, her fingers played at the nape of my neck at some point. We were both a bit dazed by it all—first the girl in the pillar, and now the two of us, alone here, so late at night, with the motorbikes and the oil drum, and the smell of tears, which isn't at all a nice smell, though it's one I've always liked. We didn't kiss.

I felt slightly spooked as I rode home. I sometimes felt that way in the dark, when the bridge loomed behind me. There had been two suicides that year, though neither had been found in Ludwig's garden. The first had landed close to the river, and the other had fallen through the glass roof of an agricultural machinery repair shop on the right bank. It was the fourth time in twelve years that roof had been smashed—the owner must have been pretty annoyed. And now there had been this girl in the pillar, so that the bridge *was* somehow alive after all, just as I had feared when I was younger. All this was going through my head—and thoughts of Vera too, of course—the feel of her hair and skin. I forgot to mention that I'd also touched her arms, where the skin was bare. I even—slowly, and only for a second or two—pushed two fingers up the short sleeves of her dress.

I wondered for a long time whether I should tell Ludwig about this encounter in the workshop. Things are never easy between brother and sister, and perhaps he'd have taken it the wrong way. There had been a funny atmosphere that day—we couldn't stop thinking about the girl in the bridge. I was sure Ludwig would have understood in the end, but I kept quiet all the same. By then our twin project was so far advanced, I think, that we no longer had to talk about everything. We knew or guessed the important things about each other.

◆

A few days later, it emerged that one of the two kidnappers had been a father from our school. I can still remember the look on the boy's face when his mother came to pick him up. His father had already been arrested and the news had spread like wildfire, so that everyone sitting out on the front steps knew what had happened. We expected the boy to cry, or at least look ashamed, but as he strode out of school between us, he held his head high, like a king. His mother was crying.

We discussed the scene at length when we went to the Greek taverna after school. We went to the taverna a lot, because it had the best pinball machine in town. Space Patrol, it was called. They all had names like that, but this one was the best—none of the others gave you such an intense display of sounds and lights. It blinked and beeped and flashed and rattled—like a real space battle, maybe—and we shot the little metal balls into the maws of intergalactic beasts who probably all had their eyes on the busty blond girl in the high boots—high boots and three red stars covering the vital spots, nothing else. We drank a glass of water each but never ordered anything to eat, so the Greek landlord always gave us sour looks when he saw us coming. But how could we have eaten yeeros or moussaka or tzatziki? We rowed in the lightweight class and weren't allowed to weigh more than 125 kilos between us. We managed without starving ourselves, but we didn't eat fatty food. I'm afraid I found it easier to keep my weight down than Ludwig did. Though we'd eaten the same quantities of the same foods all winter, by the summer Ludwig was having to restrict himself a bit. So we played pinball and talked about the kidnapper's son, though Ludwig didn't have much to say for once. I got worked up about how untroubled by it all the boy had seemed—I suppose Ludwig saw no point in saying anything because he agreed with everything I said.

◆

Ludwig didn't turn eighteen until the autumn, and I had to wait until the winter, so neither of us had a driver's licence. That meant we couldn't drive ourselves to the regattas. My father took us—he'd been driving us ever since our first regatta, when we were twelve and rowed in a quad. 'Next time it's my dad's turn,' Ludwig had said. Not long before the race, he rang and said his dad couldn't make it, but he was sure he'd give us a lift the time after. It went on like that for a while—Ludwig could give very longwinded explanations as to why it was impossible for his dad to take us that particular weekend. Eventually, though, he dropped the subject.

I never saw Ludwig's father at a regatta, but it didn't matter, because my father was keen not to miss a single one. What was annoying, though, was having to sit in the car with him, especially once he'd remarried. His new wife was a colleague from the curtains section of the department store where he was assistant manager in charge of household goods. On the sometimes long car journeys, the two of them talked at length and in minute detail about the department store, so that by the time we got home we knew all about cutlery sets and Tupperware—and all about the people who bought and sold cutlery sets and Tupperware. My poor father.

I had no trouble, then, understanding why Ludwig had started to think about alternatives. On the Friday before the fifth race of the season, he rang to say we wouldn't be going with my dad—I should ride my bike round to his place on Sunday morning. It wasn't exactly easy to explain this to my father. I was vague and a bit cryptic, but he didn't quiz me for long before announcing that he'd come along all the same. I think he was very proud of me. We'd beaten the twins from Potsdam in the first four races. It was an important season for us, because the regional championships were to be held on our reservoir at the end of the summer.

That Sunday I rode my bike round to Ludwig's first thing. He was waiting in the garden. His parents' car wasn't there—they liked to take city breaks on the weekend.

'Dream anything?' Ludwig asked.

'No,' I said. 'Did you?'

He shook his head.

What I'd said wasn't altogether accurate. I'd dreamed I was lying on my belly on the beach with someone sitting on my bum, trickling hot sand onto my back as I watched a pod of whales swim by out to sea. For a long time I didn't know who it was sitting there, but when I was pretty much covered in sand, a face popped up next to mine and it was Vera.

Ludwig led me into the workshop, where two motorbikes were parked, one without a gearbox and the other a recently restored silver Triumph. The Triumph looked like new and had two white helmets and two black leather jackets lying on the saddle. Ludwig rubbed his hands together gleefully.

'Your dad will throw us off the bridge,' I said.

He grinned and put on one of the jackets, so I did too, and then we helped each other fasten the helmets. As we pushed the motorbike out onto the road, I saw Vera standing at a window. Ludwig kicked the starter twice. I'd always liked the sound of the older motorbikes, a hollow gurgle that was almost a moan, like a distress call—in neutral, at any rate. The rest of the time they shrieked in a way that sounded pretty hysterical. It felt unbelievably good, driving through the country with Ludwig. A motorbike was just right for us. It's a vehicle made for two—you move in unison, tilting forwards when you brake and backwards when you accelerate, leaning into the bends together when you turn right or left.

Ludwig drove up the hill carefully, but at a fair speed, then onto the motorway and over the bridge. Looking down at the valley on either side, I whooped with joy. The sun was low in the sky and the river glinted like a narrow strip of tinfoil. On the way to the regatta, all went well, and the race was a success—we narrowly beat the twins from Potsdam—but on the way back, we were stopped by the police, who appeared behind us from out of nowhere. They gave a brief blast on the siren and Ludwig pulled over to the right, stopped and immediately dismounted. The police parked a few metres further back. Then something happened that still brings me out in goose flesh when I think of it.

I too had dismounted, and an almost imperceptible ballet began. Taking small steps, we moved in silence towards one another and past one another, crisscrossing and circling, apparently haphazardly. By the time one of the policemen had reached us, I was the one standing at the handlebars. Ludwig and I were wearing the same helmet and similar jackets. We were the same height, the same build and we were both blond.

'Can I see your driver's licence, please?' the policeman said to me.

'I don't have one,' I said.

I don't want to go into detail about what followed. It wasn't so hard to deal with, because we shared the burden. Ludwig had to live with his father's anger, while I got twenty hours' community service. I worked it off at a municipal garden, transplanting trees, loosening soil. I had no trouble coping with the physical work—what was unpleasant was the company, a motley crew who'd been done for assault, talked only of violence and threatened each other with the knives we'd been given to prune shoots. It was awful, but I got through it all right because I knew it would have been much harder for Ludwig than it was for me. Sometimes he had trouble keeping his mouth shut—a frankness which may have been a strength, but could have triggered a life-and-death battle in the municipal garden. *Maybe*, I would think, after hours of gory tales and dark threats, *maybe right now I am saving Ludwig's life*. Then I would find the strength to go on.

◆

Not much else happened in the weeks following our motorbike ride. The next thing worth mentioning took place on an evening exactly like so many others back then. We had dinner with Ludwig's father and Vera—his mother worked late shifts, and I didn't often see her. We ate in silence—there never was much talking in that family at the best of times, and there was still tension in the air. Ludwig's father had bought half a dozen U-locks and locked up all the roadworthy motorbikes. The bill had gone to Ludwig.

After dinner, we went up to Ludwig's room and listened to the radio. We did that a lot at the time. Ludwig had sold his television and stereo to pay for the locks—his father had been merciless. Now Ludwig had an old dark-wood tube radio in his room. The speaker in the middle was made of pale wicker, and the dial glowed green. Best of all was the heavy tuning knob, so sensitive that you could get all the stations with a single turn of your wrist. The sound was muffled, but we had such fun sending the red pointer on its travels that we didn't mind.

Soon we had listened to several stations and found two favourite programs. The first was early on a Saturday afternoon and broadcast live test drives—two men driving around the country in a new car, discussing its strengths and weaknesses. The drive always incorporated a so-called vibration track, and we would laugh ourselves silly when the two old men gave the car a thorough shake-up as they tried to rate the shock absorbers. Their words came out jerky and disjointed, and we decided that they were the best rappers in Germany. The other show was called *Roots, Rock and Reggae* and presented an episode in the history of reggae every Monday evening. We liked the music and sometimes even danced. I don't want to keep going on about this, but it was another sign of how far we'd progressed. Dancing didn't come half as naturally to the boys our age as it did to the girls, and so there was something special about the moment when, one evening, without a word, we got up at almost exactly the same time and began to dance to the reggae—separately, and yet together.

I left after midnight, once the show was over. The light was still on in the workshop. That was nothing unusual, and I'd got into the habit of looking to see who was there as I passed. I suppose it started the night the girl was found in the pillar. It was usually Ludwig's father, kneeling at a motorbike, tightening bolts or laying Bowden cables. He had a slow, calm way of doing these things. He too often had a radio on, a small transistor hanging from the ceiling by a wire, but it was always people talking, never music.

Thinking back, I remember another sound I associate with the workshop—a hum coming from the fluorescent lights. It's less the hum I remember, though, than the crackling noise and the brief sizzle when a moth came too close and scorched itself. The lights were always swarming with insects in the summer, and there was a fair amount of crackling and sizzling. The more I think about it, the clearer I can hear the sounds of the workshop—the voices from the radio, the humming, the crackling and sizzling—and a click when Ludwig's father knocked his spanner against a cylinder. He often had his back to me, in which case I'd go silently on my way to the garden gate, where my bike was leaning against the fence. If he saw me, he gave me a brief nod and went back to tightening bolts. It was strange, but he never entirely lost a certain awkwardness towards me.

It wasn't Ludwig's father in the workshop that day, though, but Vera. She was sitting on the stool with the greasy cat in her lap, stroking its head.

'I think he's sick,' she said when she saw me.

I took a step into the workshop.

'What's the matter with him?' I asked.

She shrugged.

I went over to her and crouched beside her. I stroked the cat's back; it opened its eyes for a second. 'Poor cat,' I said.

Its coat was quite hard, matted with oil. It gave a short, dry cough. I stroked its back, starting at its neck, while she stroked its head. Inevitably our hands touched, but only a few times, and only briefly.

I've forgotten exactly what happened next. It's funny what we remember and what we don't. I remember, for instance, that Vera was wearing a navy blue dress with a pattern of little yellow flowers, but I don't know if the cat jumped off her lap or she gently shooed it away. What I am sure of is that we ended up facing one another, standing very close—holding one another, in fact. The dress had a zip, a long zip, going all the way down her back. *Don't undo it*, I kept thinking. *Don't undo it, don't.* I undid it, and it made a wonderful noise. Vera stood very still, her eyes closed. She wasn't wearing a bra. My hand—my right hand, I think—was on her ribs, just beneath her armpit, my middle finger touching the short, thick, curly hair there, as my thumb drifted down in a slow, careful arc. When you run your thumb very slowly over someone's skin like that, you feel all the little hairs and realise they're everywhere, though you can't see them. I've never felt anything as fine as the downy hair on Vera's skin. My thumb found the curve of her breast, and my other fingers followed. The skin there was so soft—sometimes I can still feel it, even now. *No, no, that's enough, don't go any further, you mustn't*, I told myself, but there was no stopping my hand as it drifted on, following the curve, until it met a nipple as hard as a small stone, and there the *no* shattered, splintering into a thousand pieces. Vera drew in her breath sharply. I heard the sizzle of a bug zapped by the light.

◆

We took one of the blankets Vera's father laid over the motorbike tanks so he wouldn't scratch the paintwork when he was tinkering about with the engines and walked to the end of the garden, where the wood began. It was different from with Josefine. We undressed separately, facing away from one another. When I turned around, Vera was kneeling on the blanket, her hands folded in front of her crotch. She didn't want me to touch her. She straddled me, taking my penis and lowering herself onto it until just the tip was inside her. She moved slowly on top of me for a while, then took a little more of me inside her and again moved for a while on top of me while I lay there, waiting for her to take more. When I was right inside her, she suddenly froze, and everything went quiet. I saw her thighs quivering, but she didn't make a sound, and then she dropped down on me and sank her teeth into my neck. I cried out, and though I've often tried to remember, I don't know to this day whether a truck rumbled over the bridge at that moment, drowning my cry, or whether the sound reverberated into the night.

Afterwards she lay beside me. It was a warm night. We looked up at the bridge, listening to the whistle and rush of the cars and watching the lights. We didn't say much. Maybe we didn't say anything at all.

4

In the middle of that summer, something beautiful happened. When I went round to Ludwig's one day, he was in the workshop, which was unusual. There he was in a corner, kneeling in front of a scarlet Triumph T20 Tiger Cub, one of the oldest motorbikes there, a rusty 1959 model. The stuffing was bursting out of the saddle, the wires and Bowden cables were frayed, and it had a damaged piston. The owner had brought it to be fixed years ago and hadn't been seen since. Some said he'd run away from the responsibilities of fatherhood.

Others said he'd ended up under a bus.

Ludwig was removing the front mudguard when I arrived. I went over to him and watched him struggling with the spanner. One of the bolts had rusted fast and he couldn't get a purchase on it. I could tell from the look on his face that he'd been trying for some time. I also knew he hadn't asked his father how you undid a rusty bolt, though he was there in the workshop too, holding a dark plastic mask with a small window to his face as he welded a frame. When he'd finished his welding, I went and asked him how you undid a rusty bolt. He fetched a yellow can with a red valve and told me it was rust remover—it would do the job in half an hour max. He didn't look at me. I took the can, went back to Ludwig's motorbike and sprayed all the rusty bolts. We spent the afternoon taking the Triumph to pieces. Ludwig didn't say he'd begun to overhaul it so that we'd have a motorbike when he and I turned eighteen later in the year. He didn't need to. It was a brilliant idea.

We started to spend a lot of time tinkering in

the workshop, and as we worked, we pondered what we'd do when we left school. We wanted work we could do together, of course, but it wasn't easy to find anything that appealed to us.

'University's boring,' said Ludwig, as we removed the cylinder head from the cylinder, and he was, of course, absolutely right. We didn't want to waste any more of our lives sitting in musty rooms while outside, in the real world, time overtook us. We racked our brains for a while until Ludwig suddenly said, 'We'll build a tower in Asia.'

I knew at once where he was coming from. There had been a lot of reports on how even young people could make heaps of money with real estate in Asia, and there was no reason we couldn't give it a go.

No sooner was the idea voiced than we began to dream up a project of our own—though 'dream' is probably the wrong word, because we took it all very seriously and didn't for a second doubt that we'd actually build our tower. We gave careful thought to the location. We rejected Seoul and

Manila, thought long and hard about Saigon and eventually agreed on Hanoi, because Hanoi was not yet too developed—it had potential. Our tower would be the tallest in the world, of course, and that meant at least 450 metres. It was to be a round tower that tapered towards the top, like a chimney, and we wanted it built in red brick with non-reflective windows—not big windows, but plenty of them. We envisaged a classically handsome building, with flats and offices. Ludwig drew the tower in engine oil on a newspaper, and we hung the drawing in our corner of the workshop.

It was wonderful talking about our Asian tower as we inserted spokes into the wheel rims or adjusted cogs in the gearbox. We stayed in the workshop far into the evening, listening to bugs and gnats sizzle on the fluorescent tubes, and talking and talking. The top floor would be our office, of course—an immense loft, 450 metres above Hanoi, above the world.

'We'll have the most stunning secretaries you can imagine,' I said.

'At the top of a tower like that, anything is possible,' said Ludwig.

We spent a lot of time working out the best way to power our lift, because it had to be fast, of course—as fast as lightning, the fastest in the world. We wondered about jets, about rockets—it was glorious. Building in Hanoi wouldn't cost much, so getting hold of money for the construction would be a cinch. There were shares, the internet, millions of possibilities—and the banks would cough up the balance. Other people managed, didn't they, and there were two of us. We were twins—together, we could do anything.

◆

I'm afraid, though, that Ludwig's mood grew worse over the course of that summer. Even when working on the motorbike, he was bad-tempered and unusually taciturn—it was only the imaginary building work on our tower in Asia that seemed to cheer him up a bit. Once the topic was exhausted—once we'd agreed, for instance, that we'd give preference to stockbrokers, modelling agencies and private military contractors when letting the offices—he fell to brooding.

I have a clear recollection of sitting with him on the grass one day, removing rust from the brake and clutch levers. All of a sudden, he stopped, looked at the brake lever and said, 'Isn't it strange that somebody's life can depend on a stupid bit of metal like this? I mean, you pull it at the wrong moment, or you don't pull it at all, and wham! Funny, eh?' He went back to his sanding. He was right, of course, and as he said it, the thought seemed as familiar to me as if I'd thought it myself at that same instant. That was normal for us—it happened all the time—and yet I began to worry about him.

There was no overlooking the growing trouble he was having maintaining our ideal weight. He ate only two-thirds of what I ate, at most, and yet he felt permanently hungry. That, I think, was the main reason for his bad mood. Never being able to eat enough can be punishing, as I'd later discover for myself. It was probably the combination of eating so little and training such a lot that was getting him down. We'd stopped going to the taverna altogether.

'Just the smell of that Greek shit is enough to make you fat,' he said.

It was a surprise to us both when we lost the regatta in the neighbouring town. The twins from Potsdam overtook us in the final spurt, beating us by half a length, and we stepped up our training.

Training and tinkering—that's how we spent our summer. It was a lot of work to get the old Triumph back in shape. We spent hours scratching rust from the paintwork with wire brushes, took parts to be painted, chrome-plated, upholstered, got hold of new pistons, new cylinders. I often went to Ludwig's father to ask his advice, and he was always glad to give it. If anything, his answers to my questions were sometimes far too detailed. But he never gave us any practical help, never touched our bike. It was as if someone had chalked a line around our corner of the workshop, and Ludwig's father knew not to cross it.

◆

Around this time Ludwig started to get funny if he thought I was spending too much time with anyone else. We spent almost every waking minute together as it was, but I did sometimes ride home at lunchtime to eat with my mother, who was very lonely. It wasn't long after our defeat, I think, that Ludwig asked me whether this was really necessary—whether it wasn't driving a wedge between us and making it harder for us to grow together. I'd been wondering about that too and had come to the same conclusion. Besides, it wasn't exactly pleasant having lunch with my mother, because she was always going on about my father, though apparently without the least resentment. You'd have thought from the way she spoke that she was expecting him back for dinner at the latest—and looking forward to it. I found this hard to cope with, so I'm sure I was right to abandon that particular routine.

My mother insisted, though, that I sleep at home during the week. 'Until you're eighteen,' she said. That put Ludwig in a foul mood. He'd suggested moving a second bed into his room—a good suggestion, and a very reasonable one. It would, of course, have been wonderful to talk about our Asian tower just before we drifted off, in that sleepy state where you're almost dreaming and it's so much easier to give free rein to your fantasies. By then we'd decided to make the tower five hundred metres, to make it harder for anyone to outdo us. Our flag would fly from the top.

Our work on the Triumph was going well. We'd got all the parts working again or bought new ones, and now we began to rebuild it. It was incredibly satisfying, hanging that gleaming engine in its newly painted frame and screwing it tight. Over time we'd become good mechanics and hardly needed Ludwig's father's advice anymore. When Vera came into the workshop, she and I only gave each other a brief nod. She stayed at the front with her father, watching him work.

◆

Ludwig usually went to bed at about midnight, after we'd listened to the radio for a bit. When I was sure his father had knocked off for the evening, I'd leave the house and head for the workshop, where I'd be sure to find the light on. Since our first time together, Vera often waited for me—in fact, come to think of it, she waited every night. As soon as she saw me, she'd throw her arms around my neck and start kissing me. I felt a bit uncomfortable about this—the workshop was a place I shared with Ludwig—but I let it happen.

We never spoke until after we'd had sex. I didn't do much talking even then, but Vera talked a great deal. I liked listening to her. Sometimes the cat came and sat on the grass just near where we were lying and looked at us. Cats look so severe when they sit up straight and still like that—so stern, almost reproachful—and there was no ignoring Otto. It was no use just looking away—his oily smell carried to us on the breeze.

Vera seemed a little taller every time I saw her—she was still growing. She wanted to be tall, but more than anything she was waiting for her breasts to fill out. Sometimes it happened late, she said, cupping first her right breast and then her left.

'Do they seem bigger to you?' she asked.

'I think so,' I said.

'Feel,' she said.

I put my hand on her right breast and then on her left one.

'Yes, a bit,' I said.

'You're lying,' she said. 'It doesn't matter if they don't grow any more. The main thing is that they're a nice shape.'

'Yes,' I said.

'Do you think they're a nice shape?' she asked.

'Very nice,' I said, and it was true. They were almost perfectly round. They weren't the kind of breasts you could lay your head between, but they felt nice—firm but yielding. Besides, I liked her mole.

'If they grow some more, I'll have a perfect figure,' said Vera. 'Not many girls have long legs and big breasts.'

'You already have a perfect figure,' I said.

'True,' she said. 'But who cares, anyway? Do you know what? I want to come and live in your tower in Asia too.'

It was always the same with her. After we'd done it, she only ever lay quiet for a moment, then something would pop into her head and she'd start chattering away. I couldn't just lie on the blanket and listen to her, though, because she always had so many questions.

'How high is it going to be now?' she asked.

'Five hundred metres,' I said.

'How much higher than the bridge is that?'

'I don't know,' I said. We looked up at the bridge. I liked watching the white shimmer of the headlamps, moving like streaks of light. 'Maybe eight times as high,' I said.

'I want the floor down from you,' she said, 'the second-highest. You boys have to live right at the top, of course, no question of that.' She could be quite cheeky. 'But do you know what? I think your tower's going to be too gloomy—dark red bricks and such small windows. Why are you making it so gloomy?'

'Don't know,' I said. 'We like it like that.'

'Oh well,' she said, 'maybe I'll tie a bow around my floor—a yellow one. How long do you think the ribbon would have to be?'

'Don't know,' I said. I didn't want a bow around our tower in Asia.

'My floor's going to be amazing,' she said. 'I've got it all planned out. No walls—not a single wall, not even around the toilet—and hardly any furniture. Just a bed, a cupboard, a table and a chair—but loads of flowers and plants. Do they have ivy in Hanoi? Ivy would be great. We could grow it up the tower—it wouldn't look so gloomy all covered in green. And I'd like tortoises,' she went on, 'lots of tortoises. I'd let them go wherever they liked, in and out of the flowers and plants—what do you think?'

'Why tortoises?' I asked.

She straddled me.

'They're so slow,' she said.

A little later the questions started up again: 'Will you come and visit me on my floor?'

I didn't like that. The tower in Asia was something between Ludwig and me. I didn't mind Vera daydreaming about it—I even liked the thought of her living up there with her plants and tortoises, nearly five hundred metres in the air. But I didn't want her talking about the tower and me in the same breath. I can't remember how I answered her question—or if I answered at all—but I don't think she persisted, because I pulled her down to me and kissed her breasts. Maybe she even bit me. She never could resist biting me just as I was starting to revive, and I rarely managed to suppress a cry. Sometimes it was swallowed by a truck, and sometimes it wasn't.

◆

There'd been a few things I had to get straight with Vera right from the start. After our first time it was funny seeing her in school the next day, especially as I was with Ludwig when she walked past. We gave each other a nod as we always did, and I was glad it was over and done with, everything back to normal. That made it all the more annoying when fat Flavia, Vera's best friend, handed me a note in the morning break. Ludwig wasn't around. *Meet me at lunchtime?* it said on one side of the paper, and *Physics lab* on the other. I didn't go. I wasn't having any of that. You had to keep things separate. I think I managed to make that clear to her. We only met on nights when spending time with her meant giving up sleep, not giving up my time with Ludwig. I don't see that anyone could have objected.

Vera often surprised me. One night, for instance, after telling me a bit about her friend Flavia, she said, 'It's really nice with Flavia too.'

'What?' I said.

Vera kissed me tenderly on the lips, and just then it started to rain, rather suddenly. We hurried into our clothes, I gave her a kiss and we went our separate ways. On the wet bike ride home, I thought a lot about what Vera had said and about her kiss. Did that mean she'd been with Flavia too? To be honest, I found it hard to imagine—Vera in bed with her fat friend. I knew it wasn't as weird when it was girls as it would be for us, but the next time with Vera was a bit strange—I kept seeing her with fat Flavia instead of me. I'm not saying the thought was entirely unpleasant, just slightly bizarre. Afterwards I asked her whether she was really sleeping with Flavia *and* me.

'I don't *sleep* with you,' she said. 'We do it on a blanket under a bridge.'

She really could be quite cheeky. But I didn't mind. I gave no more thought to Flavia—or only every now and then.

◆

I'm afraid there was an ugly scene one day, a scene I don't like to describe, but it was part of that summer and can't be left out. Ludwig and I had been training hard and were so exhausted that we caught the riverboat home instead of riding our bikes. We sat side by side on a bench at the front, letting the wind cool us, one of those moments when you're too tired to speak but don't need to, each understanding perfectly how the other feels. But when we got back to the house under the bridge and went straight to the workshop, we saw something we'd never seen before: Vera was sitting on our Triumph, twisting the throttle grip, which wasn't yet connected to the carburettor.

Remembering what happened next makes me shudder. Ludwig rushed across the workshop, grabbed his sister by the shoulders and tore her off the Tiger Cub, knocking it over on top of her. That turned out to be lucky, because it gave her at least some protection from the blows—and, I'm sorry to say, kicks—inflicted on her by her brother. If it hadn't been for their father, who was in the workshop gutting an exhaust pipe, I'd never have got Ludwig off his sister. I dragged him outside, and on the grass beside the workshop he lunged at me. Too well matched, we wrestled for ages, neither of us able to get the better of the other, until finally, simultaneously, we gave up. We soon made it up, deciding that the length and intensity of our fight were further evidence of how alike we'd become.

Looking back, I don't think there was anything so unusual about Ludwig's attack on Vera. Things often get pent up between brother and sister and then suddenly erupt, and such incidents can seem worse at first sight than they actually are.

◆

The further the summer went on, the quieter things grew between Ludwig and me. For one thing, the assembly work demanded a great deal of concentration, and for another, Ludwig really wasn't in a good way. I did all the talking and all the work while he sat cross-legged next to the Triumph, watching me. If I turned to look at him, I'd see that it wasn't my hands he was watching as I filed and hammered—it was my face.

I can recall only one thing Ludwig said around that time, but it was so apt that it was almost poetic. 'A motorbike,' he said, 'is like a coxless pair. Two lives, one fate.'

'That's what makes it so perfect for us,' I added, and I seem to remember feeling almost touched.

The day I put in the manifold and the exhaust pipe, neither of us had spoken for over an hour when it occurred to me that it was a long time since we had last talked about our tower in Asia. Not wanting to lose sight of our project altogether, I suggested putting in an underground car park beneath the tower—the deepest underground car park in the world. Ludwig liked that kind of thing, and he seemed very bad-tempered lately— he needed cheering up. So as I tried to screw the exhaust pipe to the manifold—a fiddly business because the parts weren't a perfect match—I told him that our underground car park would need forty levels, because there'd be so many people living and working in the tallest tower in the world.

'Forty levels,' I said, doing the sums out loud, 'would go at least a hundred and forty metres into the earth—it would mean digging a really enormous hole.'

What appealed to me the most, though, was the thought of driving all the way up from the bottom. Even in regular multistorey car parks I loved those

hairpin bends connecting the levels and the thrill
you got in your belly, driving up and down.

I think I had just told Ludwig how we'd ride
our Triumph all the way from the lowest level up
to the top—at high speed, of course—when he
suddenly interrupted me.

'Stop it,' he said. 'Stop going on about that
stupid fucking tower.'

I felt slightly hurt to begin with, but I soon
realised he was right—the tower was a childish
idea we'd outgrown. He didn't have to say it the
way he did, but he was hardly eating at the time. In
spite of his diet, he was usually a kilo or two heavier
than me before the regattas and had to sweat off
the excess weight—go jogging with two tracksuits
on, one on top of the other, and then finish off in
the sauna. We'd won one regatta and lost the next.
After that there were only three weeks to go until
the regional championships on our reservoir.

We didn't mention the tower again for a
while, though Vera sometimes talked about it,
chattering away about her plants and tortoises, and

dithering between a yellow bow and a green one. I never bothered replying. I have a feeling I was pretty grumpy and uncommunicative myself at the time.

◆

It was my poor mother who had to bear the brunt of my moods. She only ever got to see me at breakfast—by the time I got home at night, she'd long since gone to bed. She'd recently begun to snore slightly, which I knew because she always left the door to her room ajar. Until I got back, she only half slept. 'I get worried,' she told me at breakfast on more than one occasion, and there was no mistaking the reproach in her voice. I said nothing. I can't remember a word of what I might have said to my mother back then. It's possible I didn't speak at all. She was working in the department store again, but in ladies' clothes, not curtains. She often saw my father and his new wife in the canteen, and sometimes they had coffee together. That annoyed me. Most of what my mother said annoyed me. It began first thing in the morning with *Johann, time to get up*, her voice all nice and kind, and her hand stroking my cheek as she said it.

I do remember seeing her once at about three in the morning. I'd been with Vera and hadn't long been asleep when I was woken by the phone. I jumped straight out of bed, because it could only be Ludwig—and it was. He'd sometimes rung me at night in the past when he'd had a sudden thought he couldn't keep to himself—that we ought to build our Asian tower in Rangoon, the capital of Burma, for instance, rather than in Hanoi. But it hadn't happened for a while.

'Johann,' he said, 'get dressed and come round right away.' He sounded wide awake.

'Has something happened?' I asked, but it was a stupid question. I could hear that nothing bad had happened. I even thought I detected excitement in his voice.

Just then my mother came out of her bedroom. *Has something happened?* her eyes asked. She was wearing striped pyjamas, and her hair was so thin,

I wondered whether she wore a wig during the day, and I suddenly felt sorry for her. Perhaps I felt sorry for myself, too—I'm not sure. I didn't want an old mother, but I knew then that was exactly what I had. After years of not caring how old our mothers and fathers were, it had recently started to matter to us. Anyone with young parents had acquired a certain kudos, perhaps because we assumed that young parents were like friends—or just less embarrassing. We were of an age when parents were almost permanently embarrassing. If someone had a party, for example, you could be sure that their parents would soon turn up and start dancing. They would dance differently from everyone else and wouldn't notice how embarrassing they were. I saw an awful lot of parents dancing at parties and the looks on their children's faces. It was painful, especially when the parents were old. My mother spared me that, but she did, as I realised that night, have extremely thin hair. I resolved not to be seen with her anymore. We really could be very cruel at times.

As Ludwig kept talking, I tried to reassure her with looks and gestures.

'Okay,' I said in the end, and hung up. 'That was Ludwig,' I told my mother. 'He'd had a sudden thought.'

'At three in the morning?' she asked.

'It's all right, Mum,' I said. 'Go back to bed.'

Isn't it strange that a time comes when you start sending your parents to bed? And isn't it even stranger that they obey you? My mother went to the toilet and then to bed. I got dressed and waited in my room until I heard her soft snores.

Ludwig met me at the garden gate. I could see straight away that he was looking much more cheerful than he had in a long time. He took my bike and pushed it into the garden.

'At last,' he said.

'What's going on?' I asked.

'Come with me,' he said. 'Something's happened.'

He led me to the other end of the garden at a kind of jog. There, at the edge of the wood, I could see somebody lying on the ground. I stopped. *Vera*, I thought. It was clearly a human body, but it wasn't moving.

'Ludwig,' I said, 'what is it? Who's that lying there?' I almost asked: *What have you done?* but I knew immediately that he wouldn't do such a thing. He was my brother.

'Come on,' he said. 'Come closer.'

'Who is it?' I asked.

'I don't know,' said Ludwig.

'Is she…is he dead?' I asked.

'Dead? Yes, of course. Come on.'

I took two steps towards the body and saw that it was a man with short hair, smaller than us. He wasn't really lying—he was huddled up with his face to the ground, one leg folded beneath his body, the other stretched out behind him. His bum was slightly raised and his back arched more sharply than you would have thought possible.

'He jumped half an hour ago,' said Ludwig. 'I heard him land and came straight out. The others are asleep.'

'Are you sure he's dead?' I asked.

'Anyone jumping from up there has to be dead,' he said.

I looked up and saw streaks of light flash by as cars flew over the bridge.

'Have you rung the police?' I asked.

'Just look at the funny way he's lying,' said Ludwig. He took a step towards the body.

For a while neither of us spoke. A car drove west, another east.

'Come on, let's sit down,' said Ludwig, settling himself cross-legged in front of the body and leaning forward, his elbows propped on his legs, chin resting on his hands. 'What do you think his name is?'

'Don't know,' I said.

'Aren't you going to sit down?' he said, and I squatted down behind him on my haunches.

'Do you think it's a good idea,' I asked, 'to be sitting here like this when the police come?'

'Wonder why he jumped,' said Ludwig. 'Maybe his girlfriend left him, maybe he just had a boring life, maybe he was going to die anyway. Imagine being told you're terminally ill—that you'll soon be in constant pain and wheelchair-bound and all that shit.' A truck drove over the bridge. 'Though he doesn't look ill,' Ludwig said.

'When are the police coming?' I asked.

'The police don't understand this kind of thing,' Ludwig said.

'So you haven't called them.'

'I called you,' he said. We were silent. For a moment I thought the dead man had moved, but of course he couldn't have.

'Isn't it amazing, the way he's lying there?' said Ludwig. 'So quiet and still. Have you ever seen anyone that still? I haven't. Even when you're asleep, you move a bit—you breathe and snore—but this guy really is completely still.'

'Please call the police,' I said.

'Now listen,' Ludwig said, 'I've been waiting a long time for something to happen, something big. Death is a big deal, you know that. A dead man can tell us things, and I'm not going to let the police fuck that up for me. This dead man belongs to us—just us, you and me. We're going to come back and sit here some more, and things will be good for us.'

I think he said something along those lines. He was crouching in front of me, grasping me firmly by the shoulders. I nodded. He thumped me on the back with his right hand. Then he got up.

'Okay,' he said, 'you go home now. I'll sort things out here.'

I got up and had another look at the dead man. I noticed that he was wearing shorts. *Why's that? Why would a grown man wear shorts?* I wondered. I couldn't see his face, but he didn't look like a child—he was too big. Then I left. At the garden gate I turned and saw Ludwig dragging the dead man under the trees.

At school the next morning we didn't mention the dead man, but I think we both felt a certain excitement—an excitement that bound us together as nothing had before. We were the guardians of a secret, but it was not the kind of secret usually kept—or rather, flaunted—by people our age. Ours was a real secret, and we cared even less than usual when our geography teacher tied himself in knots trying to explain the current political situation in the Balkans. We exchanged glances and smiled.

After school we went for a long row and then spent the rest of the afternoon putting the wiring harness in the Triumph. In the evening we sat in Ludwig's room with the radio on. At eleven, he started listening at the door to see if his father had gone to bed at last. It was after midnight when we crept downstairs. I was worried Vera might be waiting for me in the workshop, and the light was indeed on. But Ludwig didn't see it, or else he saw it and thought his father was still tinkering about after all.

We walked to the edge of the woods and Ludwig pulled the dead man out from the undergrowth. For the first time I saw his face. It was broad, with quite a round nose, and he was missing a few teeth. His hair covered his ears and looked strangely neat.

I wondered whether Ludwig had combed it the day before.

◆

That night we sat with our dead man until dawn. I don't want to give the wrong impression. It wasn't a solemn occasion—or only to begin with, perhaps, when Ludwig spoke of our friendship and how alike we'd become, and how important the dead man said it was that we stick together. We were twins, and now the dead man was with us too, but that made no difference except maybe to bind us even closer, because we shared him with one another and shared things were binding, whereas things you kept to yourselves drove a wedge between you.

He went on like that for the first half-hour while I, still somewhat tense, sat beside the dead man—not right beside him, but a metre or two away, cross-legged like Ludwig. I thought Ludwig had spoken well. Then the mood changed. It may seem odd, but before long we were feeling upbeat, even happy, and had to keep reminding each other not to laugh too loudly.

It began when Ludwig asked after a short pause why the dead man would be wearing shorts. He'd noticed, of course, just as I had. We always thought the same things, however ridiculous. The dead man was wearing pale corduroy shorts and even had a belt. Our fathers never wore short trousers, and neither did our teachers—none of the men we knew did, even in summer, no matter how hot it was, and we puzzled over it for a while. It's amazing how trying to work out why a man might wear shorts can lead you to imagine an entire life for him. Hot weather *might* just be reason enough for a man who spends all day out in the open, we thought—and who does that apart from builders and farmers?

We decided he was a farmer, as there were some farmers in the region and he did have a rustic look about him. That told us he hadn't had a wife, because farmers couldn't find wives these days—and that in turn told us why he'd killed himself.

He was lonely, and couldn't stand it anymore—all day in the barn and out in the fields without a wife. We were quiet for a while, because we felt sorry for him. It was sad to think of him sitting in his farmhouse in the evenings, tired from work and feeling lonely. Then one of us—I think it was me—said that the reason farmers couldn't find wives was probably that they wore shorts. We started to giggle and were soon in a silly mood we couldn't get out of.

'Men in shorts,' said Ludwig, 'always sit with their legs apart so you can see their balls, and women don't like that.'

Perhaps it seems inappropriate that we talked like that about a dead man—and in the presence of a dead man—but I didn't feel bad about it at the time and I don't today. It's just the way it was. When I think about the hysterical way we carried on that night, though, I do wonder whether the decomposing corpse wasn't releasing some kind of laughing gas.

We imagined that he'd run a small organic farm, been nice to his pigs and hadn't felt bad at all during the day, because he knew he was doing everything right and that he was a good person. But none of that was any use to him when he sat in his farmhouse in the evenings, drinking beer and watching endless football matches—even second-division games. When the phone rang, he'd think maybe it was the blond he'd met at the local dance, but it would only be the vice-president of the Livestock Association. Ludwig's voice cracked slightly as he said that, and he may even have had tears in his eyes.

I felt very much at ease sitting there next to the dead man with Ludwig. I didn't want the night to end, especially once we'd brought the dead man to life and begun to imagine him living with us. We planned to take him with us to our tower in Asia—he'd be useful there, because farmers are good handymen. It was hilarious imagining him as the caretaker in our tower, running up and down the stairs in his shorts and shooing the little Vietnamese people along in front of him. We liked him and were able to put him to good use.

We hardly noticed it getting light, but eventually we realised that the traffic on the bridge had grown heavier. We'd been lying on the grass, not talking, for an hour, each of us thinking his own thoughts. They were probably the same thoughts, pleasant thoughts of our future. When it was almost properly light, Ludwig dragged our farmer back into the undergrowth.

I'm afraid that our dead man began to smell the following night. It had been hot during the day and didn't cool down properly in the evening. He gave off a sweet, slightly nauseating smell. We tried to revive the mood of the previous night, but with that smell in the air it was hopeless. Ludwig spoke gloomily of the pointlessness of a world where you couldn't live with the dead, and despite sharing all his thoughts, I'm not sure I quite understood what he was getting at—at least not consciously. Our conversation tailed off and we sat in silence beside the dead man, who looked considerably worse than the previous night—older, much older.

'What are we going to do with him now?'

I asked as the traffic on the bridge came to life.

Ludwig said nothing, and I rode home on my bike feeling sad.

◆

When we were fitting the chain over the cogs the next day, a police car pulled up in front of Ludwig's parents' house. Because of the heat, we'd pushed the motorbike outside, where we could work in the shade. Two policemen got out and walked to the garden gate, the way policemen always walk: slowly, legs apart, faces inscrutable, as if they knew a great deal but weren't allowed to talk.

'The cops,' Ludwig called into the workshop.

His father came out, wiping his oily hands on an oily cloth. I could sense his nervousness. He walked to the garden gate and we followed him.

One of the policemen said a man had gone missing, and since there'd been several cases of people jumping and landing in this garden, they wanted to know whether we'd noticed anything unusual.

I was suddenly afraid you might be able to smell

the dead man even from the gate and began to sniff—quite loudly, Ludwig later told me, but the policemen didn't notice.

'No one's landed here,' said Ludwig's father. 'Sometimes they fall over by the agricultural repair shop,' he added.

'Would it be possible,' one of the policemen asked, 'for someone to land in the bushes over there without your noticing?'

'If anyone jumps here, we know about it,' said Ludwig's father. 'And my son always hears it when somebody jumps, even if the rest of us don't.'

'Haven't heard anything lately,' said Ludwig.

The policemen exchanged glances and I could tell that each was relieved by the other's reluctance to crawl into the bushes and look for a corpse.

'We'll ask at the agricultural repair shop then,' one of them said.

They turned to go, but Ludwig had a question. 'What kind of man are you looking for?'

'A farmer,' said the policeman who had done all the talking.

As we headed back to the Triumph, Ludwig thumped me on the shoulder. 'You see,' he said.

The following night we held a funeral for our caretaker that he couldn't have faulted. We rolled him up in an old rug and carried him to the river. There on the bank was a wide skiff we'd rowed out during the day. We stuffed a few stones from the river's edge into the rug and secured the whole thing with tape. Ludwig lit a candle, dripped some wax onto the rearmost cross brace and set the candle on it. We put the rug in the stern and rowed slowly to the middle of the river until we were exactly under the bridge. The candle flickered.

Ludwig climbed into the stern and tried to heave the rug overboard while I held the boat steady. It was a delicate undertaking—with the caretaker and the stones, the rug was pretty heavy. More than once it looked as if we might all end up in the river. In the end, Ludwig managed to get the caretaker into the water without either of us being pulled in with him, though the boat rocked like anything. For a long time we sat in silence, looking at the light of the candle flame. I didn't pray, because I didn't know how at the time.

I was very sad, as if I'd buried someone I'd really known. And somehow it was almost as if I *had* known our caretaker. I knew all about his first life, as a farmer, and all about his second life, in our Asian tower, which I presume was a happier one, because caretakers don't have such trouble finding wives, especially in Asia, where practical skills are more highly prized than over here. I think it was right to sink him in the river. He'd wanted to end his life under the bridge, and now he had found a permanent place there. Besides, he wouldn't be alone there, because we, his last friends—if, that is, he'd had any friends before us—could go and visit him every day. From then on, Ludwig was always careful to plan the intervals in our training sessions so that we could use gentle oar strokes under the bridge. I think it's fair to say that our caretaker's life had a happier ending than he might have dared hope for, but the funeral was a sad occasion even so.

When we had moored the boat to the bank again, Ludwig suggested that we go up on the bridge together. We hadn't been up there for ages and I liked the idea of going to the place where things between the caretaker and us had begun. We climbed the hill and then walked beside the crash barrier to the middle of the bridge. The river lay beneath us. We stood at the fence for a long time, thinking about our caretaker, who had stood here with all those terrible thoughts in his head, looking back at his miserable farmer's life. Nothing but fields and pigs, day after day, and so little chance of finding a wife. If he had only got to know us sooner, we could have told him about our gloomy but wonderful tower in Asia—about the work awaiting him there, and the quiet little women who are just the thing for a farmer. I'm sure he wouldn't have jumped then.

I was completely taken aback when Ludwig suddenly climbed the fence. To my horror, he threw one leg over, sat down on the top and then pulled the other leg over to join the first. His hands gripped the fence on either side of his buttocks.

'What are you doing?' I asked. 'Get down from there.'

'You come up,' he said. 'Then you'll see what the caretaker saw before he jumped.'

I didn't want to, but I couldn't stand down below while Ludwig sat up on the fence waiting for me. I climbed up, swung one leg over the top and then the other. I closed my eyes, then opened them again. What a view. It was amazing to see the valley without the fence in the way—the river directly beneath me, the lights of the little town— but I was never so terrified in my life. *One breath of wind*, I thought. *One breath of wind and you'll fly like the caretaker.* I didn't want that. I had Ludwig— I wasn't alone. I had Vera too.

'Give me your hand,' said Ludwig.

'I can't let go of the fence,' I said.

'Give it to me,' he said, slowly taking his own hand from the fence. I was sweating. 'We're twins,' said Ludwig. I loosened my hand and he grabbed it. We swayed a little, then we were still. I began to sweat even more. 'Let go of your other hand,' said Ludwig.

'Are you crazy?' I said.

'Let go,' he shouted. 'We have to do it together. I'll count to three. One...'

Never would I let go of the fence.

'Two...'

It was cold—I suddenly felt the cold. *Autumn*, I thought. *Soon it'll be autumn.*

'Three.'

I loosened my hand. Very cautiously, I glanced at Ludwig. I knew I mustn't turn my head. I knew I mustn't move. Ludwig wasn't holding on anymore either.

'We're holding each other,' he said. 'We're twins. Just you and me.'

I've no idea how long we sat like that. It felt like a long time, but in a situation like that, there's no way of knowing. Long enough, at any rate, to shake my fear. We sat on the top of the fence looking down into the valley. There was the little town, the boathouse on the reservoir, Ludwig's parents' house, the workshop where our Triumph was waiting, the river, and on the riverbed in a rug was our caretaker who had once been a farmer. But perhaps he was already in our Asian tower, changing light bulbs—who knows?

◆

I confess that I began to get worried when a whole week went by with no sign of Vera in the workshop. I started sniffing in class again, trying to get a whiff of women who'd had sex. I still love that smell like nothing else. I paid no attention to our teachers, or the writing on the blackboard, turning my head this way and that, sucking in the air until my nostrils flared, cursing soap and water and deodorant and perfume, wishing myself back in an age before people began to fight their bodily smells.

Sometimes I thought I detected something, a sour scent I associated with the half-hour after sex, and I don't think I can begin to describe the euphoria that broke over me at such moments— the exquisite sensation that crept from my brain to the tips of my toes but lasted only a few seconds before I was gripped by sadness. This girl, sitting so unassumingly in front of me, had done it last night, and I hadn't. Everyone was doing it.

I saw Vera at break, smoking cigarettes with Flavia. I didn't talk to her. I gazed at her longingly, but only when I was sure no one was watching. When she passed close to me, I pressed my lips together and breathed in through my nose until everything went black and I felt dizzy—once Ludwig had to grab my arm to stop me from falling.

'What's wrong?' he asked.

'Nothing,' I said.

◆

And then there she was, sitting in the workshop, on the stool, and when she got up and kissed me I couldn't wait—I fell to my knees, pushed my head under her dress, pulled down her knickers and pressed my face between her legs. I could feel her hand on my head through the fabric of her dress, and I stayed there like that for a long time.

I don't know what I was thinking—strange, new thoughts, I imagine.

We didn't go outside that night. Instead, I carried her to the workbench—she was so light— and set her down next to the screw clamp. She took me inside her—slowly, carefully—and this time she was the one who said *sh*, not me. While we were doing it, though, she knocked a pot of rust primer off the workbench. The lid was off, and an orange splotch spread over the floor.

I felt a little ashamed afterwards, I must admit. I was so overcome—and we often find it hard, I think, to look back at moments when we were particularly happy, because we don't recognise ourselves.

'What'll your dad say?' I asked. It was a stupid question, I know, but at such moments stupidity is our only salvation.

Since I'm being frank—and I've decided to be completely frank—there's something else I should add. As Vera was sitting there on the workbench with her eyes closed, it's possible I was thinking:

That fat friend of yours can't give you this—or rather *that obese pig*, because she really was getting heavy by then. It was mean of me, I know.

I might as well admit too that Vera had once asked me whether I'd like it if she brought Flavia along sometime.

'Why?' I asked, and I'm still slightly annoyed at myself for sounding so shocked.

'I thought men fantasised about that kind of thing,' she said, 'and Flavia's completely different from me—all soft, you know, and she has such amazing tits.'

It was strange to hear a woman talking like that—somehow I didn't feel she had the right. It was our way of talking about women.

'She likes you,' said Vera. 'I'm sure she'd come and join us, or else we could meet at her place.'

Somehow it didn't come to anything—I don't know why.

Anyway, Vera said she didn't think the orange splotch on the workshop floor would be a problem. It was strange in the workshop. It was strange not lying next to each other afterwards, and I didn't know what to do. I suppose what I really wanted was to leave. In the end I sat down on the motorbike that Ludwig's father usually tinkered about with.

'Why doesn't your dad ever come to our races?' I asked, because it was so quiet.

'Maybe he's scared,' said Vera, who was still sitting on the workbench, her legs crossed. She was smoking. She'd only recently taken it up, but she smoked quite a lot.

'Scared of what?' I asked.

'That you might lose,' said Vera.

'But why should he be scared of that?'

'Maybe he lost once too often himself.'

'Did he?'

'Don't know,' Vera said. 'He hasn't always fixed motorbikes, but I don't know what he did before— he doesn't ever talk about it.'

She came and sat pillion on the motorbike, wrapping her arms around me. I noticed that she was shivering—the nights were growing colder. 'Ride with me to the wild sea,' she said.

If the motorbike we were sitting on had had an engine, I really might have ridden off with her then and there. Her head was resting on my shoulder and she began to make soft engine noises, a low rumbling sound. I could feel her pursed lips vibrating against my shoulder, and the whole thing just seemed silly to me, but at the same time not silly at all. It was a beautiful moment, really.

'What will we do when it's winter?' she asked. 'We can't lie under the bridge when it's winter.'

I'd been wondering the same thing myself. It had been worrying me, as I didn't have an answer.

◆

There were ten days to go until the regional championships, and we'd lost the preliminary race to the Potsdam twins by a long way. Ludwig was in a state that could only be described as desperate, so I was glad when he said, 'Let's go and play pinball again.' I'd started to miss it too, and it would, of course, be a perfect distraction for him. But when we went to the taverna, something happened that came as a complete surprise to me. You might even say I was shocked.

We'd just finished the first game and had two or three sips of our water when Ludwig went to the counter and ordered not just yeeros, but yeeros with chips and tzatziki, and a Coke. He said nothing. He ate slowly, taking his time, and then he ordered ice-cream. At first I sat on a stool and watched him in silence, then I went back to playing pinball by myself and won a free game. Ludwig seemed very pleased with himself when he was finished. When we left the taverna, he bought two bars of chocolate, which he ate on the way to the boathouse.

That evening he asked his father if he'd make pancakes again, like he used to, and so his father made pancakes. The three of us sat at the kitchen table like in the old days and ate. I stopped after my first pancake, Vera after her second. Ludwig carried on eating. Vera looked at me, then at Ludwig. Nobody spoke. Their father fried pancakes, adding them to the ever-growing pile, and Ludwig ate them. I think he ate five altogether—or perhaps it was six.

◆

'What's got into him?' asked Vera when we were lying at the edge of the woods later that evening. We had two blankets with us: one to lie on and the other to cover us. Even so, it was too cold, and I no longer felt at ease under this bridge anyway, since the farmer had jumped. I kept thinking someone else was about to jump and land right next to us. I'd lost my fear of dead people, but this wasn't the time or place for a visit from one. What's more, it clearly wasn't entirely safe lying here. Who knows what happens when someone lands on you from fifty metres up?

'I don't know either,' I said in reply to Vera's question. 'At lunchtime today he just suddenly started to stuff himself.'

'I thought you had to keep your weight down,' she said. 'But let him eat. Maybe he won't always be so uptight then.'

I didn't like it when she talked about Ludwig like that.

'He's been starving himself all this time,' I said.

'He has every right to eat properly for once.'

I was in a bad mood and left soon afterwards.

◆

On the way home I was preoccupied with the thought of the last race. There were still ten days to go, and if Ludwig carried on eating like this, he'd end up over the weight limit. Sixty-five kilos was the most he was allowed to weigh, so he couldn't put on more than two and a half kilos. It might be just about all right, but it would mean that I'd have to lose exactly the same amount. If he weighed sixty-five, I couldn't weigh more than sixty, as our total combined weight couldn't be more than 125 kilos.

The next morning I skipped breakfast. My mother asked a lot of questions, and I almost thought she was going to cry. Mothers and food—that's always going to be a minefield. The first thing I ate that day was a cabbage salad at the taverna. It was seasoned with caraway and tasted good. I had a glass of water to drink. Ludwig ate moussaka and tzatziki and drank Coke. We didn't say a word, and I didn't look at him.

I starved myself for ten days, living off cabbage salad, Ryvita and apples. My stomach was an empty cave with someone clawing at the walls. It hurt all the time, and I often felt sick. After training, Ludwig sometimes had to help me out of the boat. When I didn't manage to connect the cable to the Triumph tachometer first time, I very quickly lost patience. Ludwig sat beside me, eating almond cake. His father fried pancakes for dinner, and Ludwig looked happy. Vera sometimes ate three or even four pancakes to make sure Ludwig ate at least five. She looked happy too. I drank water and ate Ryvita topped with slices of apple. As soon as Ludwig was asleep I rode home—even if the light was on in the workshop.

◆

The evening before the regatta I weighed 60.4 kilos. I put on two tracksuits and ran seven kilometres along the river. Then I had a hot bath. My mother woke me two hours later. I'd fallen asleep in the water and was cold and feverish. I barely slept.

When I stood on the official scales in the boathouse the following morning, the dial pointed to sixty. They were heavy old doctor's scales. Ludwig got on after me and they immediately tipped to the left, then stopped with a clack. The referee pushed the counterweight a little to the right and the scales came to a standstill. He pushed a little more and the dial slowly rose. It stopped at sixty-five kilos—or perhaps a touch more. But we qualified for the race.

Perhaps those ten days leading up to the race weren't our happiest—we hardly talked, and we moved more slowly than usual, one of us weak and the other bloated. But even so I have fond—very fond—memories of those days. It is true that we were moving in different directions, but even that we did in sync, so that it all came right in the end. Any weight that Ludwig put on, I lost. That, I think, can only be described as a higher level of friendship—one of the highest.

I don't want to dwell on the race. Considering our physical condition, we didn't do too badly. We led for a long time and weren't overtaken by the Potsdam twins until just before the finish. It was so close that the referees had to confer at some length. When we got out of the boat, I took Ludwig in my arms. That was unusual for us—almost unheard of, in fact. But I was happy. We'd had a difficult summer, but all in all, we'd got through it pretty well. The few times we'd hugged each other in the past—after winning a race, or when one of us had a birthday—we'd made a mess of it. We both put our heads to the same side and almost bumped noses, or else we got our hands and arms in a twist. Somehow we weren't good at it. But this hug was a success. We came together effortlessly and then stood nestled against one another on the jetty for a while. Yes, nestled against one another—why shouldn't I put it like that? It felt as if Ludwig were actually clinging to me—refusing to let go until he was ready. I think of it as one of those long embraces you see in films before one person boards a steamer and leaves the other behind.

We stayed in the showers a long time. I cupped my hands in front of my chest to catch the water and then let it run over my belly or threw it over my back. Ludwig sat opposite me, cross-legged, his head bowed, the jet of water hitting his neck. We said nothing. I hardly noticed when the others joined us, the victors noisy, the losers subdued.

◆

Ludwig didn't want me to go home with him. He said he had to revise for his driving test. I went to a kiosk, where I ate two currywursts and drank a beer, which made me tipsy. My father, his wife and my mother stood there talking, first about the race and then about the department store. It's so touching when parents make little victories out of their children's defeats. I didn't hang around for long.

In the evening I watched TV with my mother— something I hadn't done for ages. She'd cooked a stew, which we ate in front of *Crime Scene*, and I made her very happy by eating three helpings. I went to bed early and then couldn't get to sleep. I couldn't stop worrying about Ludwig. He'd been so desperate to win, and now we'd lost. He took such things very much to heart. I imagined him lying in bed, listening to the cars on the bridge and brooding. He could brood endlessly, turning some little thing over and over in his mind until it seemed so big it was overwhelming.

I think I fell asleep eventually, but soon afterwards I was woken by a strange dream. I got up and put on my clothes, slipped out of the flat, fetched my bike from the cellar and set off. I don't think I ever cycled to Ludwig's as quickly as I did that night. I hardly looked at the road, looking up at the bridge instead, trying to make out whether there was anything there, but it was a dark night and I couldn't see a thing.

At Ludwig's parents' house, I pushed open the garden gate. All was dark. The door was locked, and I couldn't get into the house. I looked to see if there was a bundle anywhere nearby—the kind of bundle the farmer had been. There was nothing.

Please, I thought, *please, please, don't jump*. It was the most horrific thing I've ever imagined: I'm walking through the garden and somebody hits the ground beside me and that somebody is Ludwig. I know now that I was being hysterical, and I should have known it at the time, but you can't always stop yourself. Isn't it worth asking, anyway, whether hysteria isn't one of our higher states of mind? It liberates us, makes us open, shows how much we care. It often looks silly, I admit, but hysterical people are actually humans at their most honest.

I climbed the hill as quickly as I could. There was nobody on the bridge. I was relieved, but continued to the middle all the same. It was a cool night and a light rain was beginning to fall, the first rain for some weeks. When I turned to walk back, I got a shock—someone was coming towards me. But it wasn't Ludwig—it was Vera.

'What are you doing here?' I asked.

'Saving your life,' she said.

That stung me, because as she approached, I'd

been thinking about how I could talk *her* out of jumping off the bridge. I had ignored the light in the workshop three times. That was no kind of reason, of course, but to have that driven home to me so bluntly gave me a jolt all the same. You don't want anyone committing suicide on your account— nobody does. But at the same time, there's no greater proof of love. Love is not, after all, diminished by unhappiness—indeed, unhappy love is often greater than the happy kind. I have since seen a lot of people I know make others unhappy to obtain proof of their love. It's a difficult topic—one I wish I could talk over with Ludwig still.

Vera said she'd seen me standing in the garden and followed me. Ludwig was in bed, she added, and she was sorry we'd lost. We walked arm in arm to the end of the bridge, and I held her hand as we climbed down the slope. I didn't have sex with her. It was too cold and wet to lie on the grass, and it wouldn't have felt right just then anyway. Under the shelter where the motorbikes were parked, she hugged me, and I could tell she had missed me. I could tell, too, that I had missed her. I told her I'd talk to my mother—that I was sure she wouldn't mind Vera staying the night sometimes. I wasn't sure that was true, but my mother was hardly going to stop me. I also said I would talk to Ludwig.

5

The next morning I was very excited. Ludwig wasn't at school because he was taking his driving test—car and motorbike. The driving test was the one we were most afraid of—more than our leaving exams, more than all the other tests and exams that lay ahead. Failing was always unpleasant, but failing your driving test was unthinkable. There was a time when it was the most embarrassing thing we could imagine—and at that age we were capable of imagining all kinds of embarrassment. Driving a car, riding a motorbike—those were things you had to be able to do.

I'd spoken to my mother at breakfast and told her I'd be having a girl round soon. She thought it was a nice idea and said she'd been wondering why I'd never brought a girl home—I was almost eighteen, after all. I let her fry me two eggs, and then filled up with toast and muesli and yoghurt.

'She'll be staying the night,' I said.

My mother, who only had coffee for breakfast, looked at me sadly over the rim of her cup, and I suddenly knew how she had looked at my father when he told her he was moving out. She said nothing, and I knew that she hadn't said anything then, either. I picked up the newspaper and began to read the sports section. I couldn't see my mother anymore, but I knew what face she was making. It was as if it was burning its way through the paper. She had these little movements she made as she raised the coffee cup to her mouth. Then she held the cup to her lips for a long time and stared over the rim into space.

◆

I skipped my last class and rode over to Ludwig's. He was crouched by the Triumph, cleaning the tank. Ludwig's father smiled when I burst in at the door, and I knew Ludwig must have passed. I was almost annoyed, because I'd wanted to hear it from him.

'Well?' I cried.

'A walkover,' he said.

I pulled him up and hugged him, but it was one of those hugs we made a mess of. We soon moved apart, each looking the other way. But as I said, it didn't mean a thing—we weren't good at it, that's all.

I was happy for Ludwig. I got him to show me his licence and give me a blow-by-blow account of the test. He told me briefly how it had gone.

'Well, how about it?' he asked.

'You bet,' I said.

The Triumph started up at the first kick. It was no surprise to hear her—we'd often left the engine running when we were fitting the carburettor and the ignition. But it was different hearing her when we knew she'd soon be on the road and that Ludwig and I would be riding her. Her gurgle was like a song we'd composed only for ourselves. She was a beauty, the most beautiful motorbike in the world. The tank was drop-shaped, the saddle flat, the tachometer set into the elongated headlamp, the single cylinder tilted slightly forward—the whole thing black and chrome and scarlet.

I helped Ludwig do up his helmet, then we set off. Right to the end, it was an amazing ride—I can't deny it. It was late summer—already autumn by the calendar, but at midday the light was still that of a summer evening, a warm, bright light—and I was sitting on our Triumph T20 Tiger Cub with my friend Ludwig, who was now also my brother, riding along narrow, unmarked roads through rolling hills dotted with black-and-white half-timbered houses, past grey-green meadows and fields of stubble, the leaves on the trees green and yellow and brown.

I remember the feeling of being on that motorbike as if it were today. I can still feel every movement, almost as if I were swaying again, the way we swayed on the bends. I hear the engine, feel the forward thrust—second gear, third gear, fourth gear—a small judder as the gears engaged, as if the Triumph were stretching. She roared along, eating up road and countryside—fourth gear, third gear, second gear. The brake gripped, the engine choked—an indignant, throaty gasp—and we slid forwards on the saddle. The motorbike seemed to grow shorter for a moment and we leant into the bend. I can still feel the thrill in my belly, though I haven't experienced it again since.

We passed through villages where people stood and stared after us, stood and listened to the sound of the engine dying away. I didn't know where Ludwig was heading—he seemed not to have a goal, but to decide which way to take at every fork. Once we stopped for a cup of coffee in a cafe garden and sat there gazing at our motorbike. I wanted to tell Ludwig about Vera, but I kept quiet—not every moment is the right moment to say something. He thumped me on the shoulder before we set off again, and I think I know what he meant. It was growing cold and I shivered a little, but I wanted to keep going, on and on forever.

◆

I've often driven back to the crossroad—I did take my driving test in the end. I park the car on a dirt track, wonder whether to get out, and then get out—I've never not got out. The road has no markings. It winds its way down the hill—just thinking about it is enough to make me sway: right, left, right, and then straight for perhaps half a kilometre to the crossroad. There are milestones, reflector posts in serried ranks like little soldiers on parade, and three trees, one on the left, two on the right—trees that I've seen in winter, spring, summer and autumn, but that were most beautiful that cold winter a few years ago, when they were covered in ice and glittered in the sun as if behind glass. Trees are usually most beautiful in autumn, of course. These three turn a yellowish red. I don't know what kind they are. They didn't obstruct the view, according to the police.

I don't bring a wreath anymore. That doesn't mean my grief has faded—it never will. There came a point when the time for wreaths had passed, that's all. Maybe I thought the crossroad should be given a second chance—that it shouldn't always be marked by death.

◆

I am, as it happens, unmarried—and not attached in any other way. I confess I have a bit of trouble with relationships. It's not that I have no luck with women—far from it. There are, after all, few places where you come across more young women than in a department store, and I can claim success even with those strangely stiff but rather beautiful creatures from the perfume department, which earns me the envy of a lot of my colleagues. That's despite working in groceries, where we don't always manage to keep our overalls clean. It's strange, when you think about it, that food and dirt should be so closely related. But I can't complain—my female colleagues like me and no one realises I limp. I've learnt to make it look as if I'm walking normally, so the only person who notices is me. I have to make a few small adjustments when I walk to force my bent bones into position. I've got used to it. I never seem to manage more than a few weeks with a woman, though. I don't know why. But what the hell, I'm all right.

Of course I miss Ludwig, but I don't want anyone thinking that means I'm always feeling down. Grief is a form of company, after all, so I'm never alone. Not that I'd ever talk to Ludwig or anything—I don't believe in any of that. It's just that I often wonder what he would have thought or done or said in a particular situation. At such times I can really be quite cheerful. I've often had to smile to myself lately when I've come across articles about cloning. I have my doubts whether scientists will ever do as good a job of getting one person to resemble another as Ludwig and I did.

What I can't get out of my head is that business with the helmet. I was conscious when I hit the road. I felt no pain, not even in my left leg, and I

saw everything that went on around me. To begin
with, though, I saw only one thing, and that was the
helmet. It sailed into view, landed on the asphalt,
bounced once, travelled a short distance, landed
again, and then rolled down the gently sloping
road—a red helmet. It crashed into a reflector post,
bounced back onto the road and spun on the spot.
A car braked and stopped just short of it. The
helmet kept spinning.

Looking back, I feel as if I lay there for hours
watching it spin. *Why is that helmet spinning over
there?* I wondered. *That's Ludwig's helmet—red
with a white stripe. He had it on his head just now.
I saw it—he was sitting in front of me. And where,*
I asked myself, *is his head? Is it still inside the helmet?
Is that possible? Is that Ludwig's head spinning
over there?*

Later I was told that I cried. It didn't embarrass
me. There were people around me. A blue light
pulsated overhead. As I was carried away, I saw
Ludwig lying on the road, his head still attached
to his body.

The helmet, and the thought that Ludwig's head might be inside the helmet—those were my worst memories of our accident. I don't remember the crash itself. As we approached the crossroad, I saw the truck coming from the left, but then I looked right. There was something there—I've forgotten what. I often wonder what it was that caught my eye, but it doesn't come back to me.

Standing at the crossroad today, I think: *Surely it has to come back to you now*—but my mind's a blank. The crossroad is set in lovely countryside, with hills and trees and a black-and-white half-timbered farm a little way off—it's very pretty. They're nice people there, too. I sometimes talk to them when I'm here—we chat about the weather and the milk yields. Little encounters like that give me a great deal of pleasure these days.

There ought to be a bench—I'm sure a lot of people would be glad to stop and rest here.

Maybe it was a hot air balloon I saw—there are a lot of hot air balloons round here. Maybe it popped up behind the trees, a big balloon with a basket hanging from it, full of people. Lovely, the lazy way they glide along. The people in the baskets like it when you wave at them, so I always do. I was surprised when Ludwig didn't brake. The truck was too close, and it had right of way. Maybe Ludwig saw the balloon too and was distracted— it's a nice, comforting thought that the last thing he ever saw was a balloon. Or perhaps he misjudged things. He hardly had any experience.

6

Vera is coming tomorrow. I haven't seen her for ages, and I'm looking forward to it, though I'm sure it won't be entirely easy, given all that's happened. After Ludwig died, we were together for another two years—good years, but difficult too. She lives in America now. She told me on the phone that she does something involving computers and has a child. I'm happy for her, I really am.

I've been over her for a long time now and have no desire to get back together, but I sometimes wonder whether it was inevitable that we broke up.

It was a pretty stupid reason, if you think about it. We were watching the news together and heard about a nasty accident that had taken place because a truck's brakes had failed—four people dead, six severely injured. For some reason I remembered what Ludwig had said when he was sanding the brake lever of the Triumph—how strange it is that somebody's life can depend on a stupid bit of metal, on whether you pull it at the wrong moment, or don't pull it at all. I told Vera about it, and when the news was over she began to ask me funny questions. When exactly had Ludwig said that? Had she and I already been together at that point? And so on. I didn't understand what she was getting at, but I answered all her questions.

'He did it on purpose,' she said later, when I was cleaning my teeth and she was sitting on the toilet.

'What?' I asked.

'The accident,' she said. 'The only reason he built the motorbike was to weld the two of you together forever. To unite you once and for all. And to take revenge on us.'

It's impossible to describe how surprised and horrified I was. An unpleasant exchange followed that I won't go into here, except to mention something I said to Vera: 'You're just jealous of what Ludwig and I had,' I said. I probably shouted. To this day I can't bear it when people speak unfairly of Ludwig. The other day, for instance, I spoke harshly to my father, when for some reason he found it necessary to remark that Ludwig had been a pretty withdrawn sort of fellow. 'You probably didn't let him get a word in edgewise with all your stories about Tupperware and pressure cookers,' I said, among other things. That shut my father up.

I soon made it up with Vera, but I don't think I ever entirely forgave her for her suspicions of Ludwig. At any rate, we were no longer happy together. Six months later, she decided to continue her studies in the States. I didn't go with her. We wrote a few times, but then we lost touch, until she rang two weeks ago to announce her visit. I'm really looking forward to it.

◆

There's a new cafe on the river these days—River Cafe, it's called. I think I'll go there with her. If the weather's fine, we could even have a swim. They say the water's been open to swimmers again since last year.